THE RESEARCH

"Men tell lies. Women tell bigger lies. And together they create hell on earth."

—*Will Swinbourne*

LAURENT BOULANGER is is the author of the critically acclaimed novel *The Girl From France,* winner of the 2014 Paris Book Festival Award for Best E-book and *Second Cut,* Winner of the 2015 Hollywood Book Festival for Best Sequel. *The Research* was made into a feature film in 2012, starring Cameron Daddo, Peter Kalos and Maria Fernandez.

THE RESEARCH

THE RESEARCH

Lighthouse

Lake Ozark Press

Copyright © 2010 Laurent Boulanger

Lighthouse is an imprint of Lake Ozark Press, Missouri, USA

Typeset in Garamond

Cover design © 2012 Lake Ozark Press

For Peter Kalos, who believed in the story.

THE RESEARCH

CHAPTER ONE

Nathan is in his mid-forties, average weight and tired-looking. He has a three-day growth. He is sitting on a green, plastic-and-metal chair in a closed-up room with a camera facing him. He wears a blue, cotton shirt and jeans. His hair is dark and almost curly.

There is a male interviewer around the same age as him behind the camera. The interviewer has a short-cropped, manicured beard and piercing, blue eyes. His beard and sideburns are dotted with grey freckles and provide him with the advantage of illusion of wisdom. He wears a casual, brown jumper and doesn't look much like a professor. In another life, he could have been an actor because of his strong visual presence—almost like electrical storm in the near distance—the type of person you can't help notice even if he's standing on the other side of the room.

Nathan doesn't really want to be in this room today, but his wife told him it was for a university research program, and the money was good even though they didn't really need the money because she worked as a solicitor, and she made enough for two. Outside, it was a lovely, sunny spring day, and whilst not particularly warm, pleasant nonetheless. He should have been outdoors looking for inspiration, or hanging around with a friend and having everlasting conversations about life and its tribulations.

He is beginning to feel self-conscious with this camera pointed at him. He doesn't like the attention, and he's never liked watching himself on film or in photographs. He straightens up on his chair and says, "Is this okay? Should I be smiling or just act normal?"

"Just be yourself," the interviewer says.

"And this is not going to be shown on television, is it?"

"No, it's just for research."

"Okay, then. Can I smoke?"

"It would be better if you didn't."

Nathan pulls a cigarette from a packet he keeps in his right shirt pocket. "I'm sorry, but I really gotta have a cigarette..."

"If you must," the interviewer says.

He lights the cigarette, takes a drag and lets the smoke out. He looks like he's having a small orgasm when the nicotine hits that soft spot. He smokes too much, and he knows it, but he doesn't care but it's the only vice he's got—other than drinking too much red wine—and he's too old to be told what to do and what not to do. He writes fiction, but he hasn't had anything published, so in one way, he does need the wine and cigarettes to sooth the hurting of not having had his creative genius recognised to this day. Most of his friends don't take him seriously because he doesn't earn any money, and in society one who doesn't earn money is more-or-less considered a bum. When strangers ask him what he does for a living, and he tells them he is a writer, they immediately want to know if he's had anything published. When he says no, he is working on his first novel, their eyes go glassy, and he knows what they are thinking—he's a bum.

The white venetian blinds around him are shut, and he can't see outside the room. He can hear traffic in the distance, but not so much it's distracting.

The cigarette smoke drowns the muskiness of the enclosed

space. The industrial, grey carpet is a little sticky, and maybe someone spilled coffee or a soft drink on it at some stage. It's not a comfortable room, right down to the injection-moulded, green plastic chair rubbing against the skin of his bottom and making it itch. He can't really see the face of the interviewer because there is spot light thrown at his face. It almost feels like he's being interrogated by the police for something he might have done, just like in those films where the cops are worse than the crooks.

He says, "God, okay, what did you want me to talk about?" He takes another drag. "She's become such a bitch lately, I think she's screwing someone else."

"Can you start from the beginning?" the interviewer says. His voice is calm and smooth, like someone in a toothpaste commercial who promises to save you thousands of dollars in future dental treatment if you brush three times a day with whatever brand of product he is inspiring you to buy.

Nathan looks intrigued. "Are you filming already?"

"Yes."

"Oh, shit!" He squashes the cigarettes in a clear but dirty ashtray on the small, wooden coffee table next to his chair. "I'm sorry, I didn't know you'd started filming. You should have said something." He notices the steady red light on the camera, a sign filming had begun.

"It's okay. We can edit later," the interviewer says.

Nathan fixes his dark, curly hair and seems much more self-conscious now. "Hello, my name is Nathan."

"You don't have to introduce yourself. You can go straight into the story."

"Ah, okay. As I was saying, she's been such a bitch lately." He pauses for a few seconds. "Can I swear?"

"You can use any language you want, it's not for broadcast."

"All right then." He focuses his gaze back at the camera. "We met at university. She was the type of woman I never thought I would fall for. You know, kind of intellectual looking with small round glasses, interesting looking. She was Italian, and I always had a deep interest in anything Italian. Something from high school, I think.

"She also seemed very confident, almost untouchable, like those Italian actors you see on TV and in films. She was older than me, and I don't know why, but I think it's also why I was attracted to her. Back in those days, I was surrounded by young women, and she just felt really exotic. I thought she was incredibly sexy."

One hour later when he is back in the streets, he can't help feeling he's been mind-raped. And now he wishes he'd never bothered, but he reassures himself it's only for ten sessions, and he promised his wife he's going to stay for the duration of the program

He walks two blocks amidst the city traffic and the throngs of people who seem to have nothing to do all day but shop and drink expensive coffees at prices that would make a homeless person cry. The sky is pencil grey, and it smells like iron and car fumes, but there is no rain predicted for the rest of the day.

Back at his apartment, his typewriter—not laptop, but a real olive green 1960s Remington—and bottle of Chardonnay are waiting for him like children who wait for parents to come home. They bring him some comfort in the knowledge that no matter how unpredictable life becomes, they will always be his, and he doesn't have to justify their existence or his dependence on them to anyone—not even to his wife.

Nathan is at the kitchen table in his blue underpants and grey tee-shirt, the clothes he had been sleeping in all night, smelling of sleep and sweat. He is smoking, a concentrated look on his face, as if his cigarette is filled with straw rather than tobacco. There is a slight discomfort on both his temples, a headache coming to life. When the day begins this way, he knows he'll probably end up with a migraine by the time he hits the pillow at night, totally exhausted from just existing.

Lucia, his attractive but older wife, is standing by the bench and is pouring freshly brewed coffee into two hand-crafted ceramic mugs—Italian made coffee, strong and a good kick up the bum first thing in the morning. She is dressed for work—gryy designer suit, white blouse, high heels, perfect make-up and styled hair. She looks Mediterranean with her olive skin and big black eyes. Her presence is charged, like a stick of dynamite with only half an inch of fuse left.

The kitchen is neat and modern with the latest European appliances and covered in white tiles like in a hospital. The smell of croissants and toasted bread fills the air and kills off the cigarette smoke. There are assorted jams and honey on the tabletop, eggs, sausages and grilled tomatoes—too much food for two people who eat three meals a day.

An uncomfortable silence sits between them.

Lucia walks with the cups of coffee and places them on the table. She bends down a little and kisses Nathan on the forehead—a ritual more than a true sign of affection.

"Are you going to be away all day?" Nathan says.

Lucia sits at the table and sips from her coffee. "I'm a solicitor—you know I have to work long hours."

He takes a sip from his coffee, but it's too hot, and he makes a painful sucking noise. He brushes his bottom lip with the tip of his right index. He knows the burn is going to irritate his lip for the rest of the day.

"Shit!" he says.

Lucia rolls her eyes. He's not sure why she's so impatient with him.

More uncomfortable silence.

He says, "Are you going to be home before ten?"

Lucia spreads butter on a French stick sliced length-way to make a toast and avoids eye contact. "I don't make the rules—

5

I work long hours so you don't have to get a shitty job and continue to work on your novel."

She dips the toast into her coffee, the way the Europeans do. She takes a bite from her toast and keeps avoiding looking at Nathan.

He is determined to get through to her. "Are you seeing someone else?"

"No."

"Look at me."

She looks at him, daringly.

"You're not seeing anyone else?"

"No, I'm not seeing anyone else."

"I rang the office yesterday at 5.30, and they said you were gone. You told me you worked until ten."

"Are you stalking me?"

"I just needed to talk to you."

Lucia turns back to her coffee and toast. Again, she purposely avoids his stare. "Do you think I'm lying?"

"I didn't say you're lying—I'm just wondering where you were."

"I had a meeting, okay?"

"Where?"

"What the fuck is it to you?"

Nathan looks notably upset. He doesn't like the f-work. His father had a potty mouth at home, and everything was f-this and f-that, and now it pinches a nerve inside every time someone says the f-word.

He stirs his coffee and thinks carefully about what his next question is going to be. "It's that young man, isn't it?"

Lucia does her best Virgin-Marie imitation. "What young man?"

"The one you talk about all the time—you don't even realise you're doing it."

"I'm working with him, for Christ's sake—of course I'm going to be talking about him."

6

Lucia finishes her toast quickly.

Nathan senses she wants to put an end to the conversation, and it somewhat convinces him she's sleeping with someone else.

He says, "You're in love with him, aren't you?"

Lucia stands up from the table, picks up her coffee and drinks it in one go. "Okay, I've had a enough of this—I'm late for work."

"Yeah, you just walk away. He's young and handsome, isn't he? You always go for young, handsome studs!"

"You're really starting to give me the shits!"

She seems really angry, but he can't tell whether it's at him, or because she hates the thought he has discovered what she's really been up to all these nights.

She storms out of the room.

Nathan is left by himself with his coffee.

He is far more upset that she could ever imagine.

He takes a puff from his cigarette and blows the smoke slowly in the direction where Lucia was sitting.

In the afternoon Nathan is having coffee with his friend Samantha. She is early thirties, dark hair, piercing eyes and a friendly smile. They are sitting at the outside terrace, protected by a barrier and umbrellas. It's been raining all morning. The rain has now stopped but the antarctic chill is still in the air. The weather is unpredictable in spring, so Nathan is wearing his favorite maroon jumper. He knows he's not much of a walking fashion statement, but he doesn't care. He is a writer, not a model. A smell of freshly-made bread from the bakery next door whisks past him.

He lights a cigarette and inhales deeply. "I know she's cheating on me," he says.

Samantha takes a sip from her coffee. "Maybe she's not—maybe you're just being paranoid."

A young, Italian-looking waiter walks up to the table. "I'm

sorry, sir, but you can't smoke here."

Nathan looks up to the waiter. "I'm outside. You're telling me I can't even smoke outside?"

"I'm sorry."

"Okay, fine."

He places the cigarette on the edge of the coffee saucer.

The waiter is about to walk off.

"Excuse me?" Nathan says.

"Yes."

"Do you smoke?"

"No, I don't—I know how frustrating it must be."

"If you don't smoke, then you don't know how frustrating it is. Why can't I smoke outside? It's not like I'm going to kill a bird or something."

"I'm sorry, sir, it's government policy."

"Government policy?" He takes his empty cup of coffee and pushes it into the waiter's hands. "Here, take this government policy and bring me another coffee. Quick, quick, hurry up."

As soon as the waiter walks off, Nathan picks up the cigarette he left on the saucer and continues smoking.. "What kind of fucked up world are we living in? Can't even have a cigarette anymore?" He can't believe he just said the f-word. He's becoming his father.

Samantha looks uncomfortable. "It's not his fault—he's just doing his job. You're so aggressive. It's not like you."

Nathan gives up with the cigarette and squashes what's left of it in the saucer. "You see, it's this whole thing with Lucia. Look what she's turning me into." He looks right past Samantha and then back at her. "I think I'm going to leave her."

"Aren't you over-reacting? It's not like you've caught them together in bed, if she's having an affair in the first place."

"I don't want to get dumped. I don't want to be the boyfriend who's going to get dumped because she's going with

8

someone half her age. Do you know how ridiculous it would make me look?"

"Just talk to her again. She is supporting you. You won't be able to sit at home and write novels all day if you separate."

"It's a relationship of convenience. Can't you understand it? I take care of the house, and she doesn't have to pay for a maid."

Samantha takes another sip from her coffee and says, "I can talk to her if you want, you know, kind of casually, and I'll be able to figure it out."

"Will you do that for me?" He thinks this over. "I think I'm going to break up tonight anyway. I just can't stand it anymore —but you still talk to her if you want."

"If you want me to talk to her, I'll talk to her."

"Talk to her." He sucks on a newly-lit cigarette like a child sucks on his last lollipop. "What about you? How come you're still single?"

She smiles instead of giving him a straight-answer.

When Nathan gets back home later in the afternoon, he works hard on his novel. But he can't do it without cigarettes and a bottle of wine. He types at the kitchen table because he doesn't have to go too far if he wants to drink or empty the ashtray. The natural light in the kitchen coming from the window is bright. When he works in the study, he feels claustrophobic. There are too many books in there and not enough light. He had been avoiding getting a real job for years because he cannot stand sitting at a desk all day, so he is aware it's kind of ironic how he ends up sitting at a kitchen table instead without the company of other office workers.

After two hours of typing away, he's exhausted, so he lies on the grey couch in the living room and channel-surfs like a teenager with attention deficiency syndrome, but nothing really interests him, just news bulletins about some war in some country he's never been to and will never visit. Re-runs of old American series. Quiz shows. Children shows. Current Affairs.

Television is a mind-killer, he believes, which is why he'd rather read a book. But he finds it hard to read and write at the same time because whatever it is he is reading ends up being partly in the novel he is writing, particularly the voice of the other writer.

It's best to not read anything at all when writing a novel, this way the only voice that comes though on the pages is his own voice. So when he takes a break, there is nothing else to do but to channel-surf, or look out the balcony of the overpriced Southbank apartment they bought three years ago and watch cars the size of ants from where he is standing.

One hour later, he's back at it, punching those typewriter keys like a madman and drinking more wine and smoking more cigarettes and filling more blank pages with black ribbon ink. He feels like Kerouac on a good day, hammering away as if his life depends on it, and in a way it does.

Before he knows it, two more hours are gone.

The writing is good—still he believes nobody will want to publish it—but the loneliness of working alone is crushing his soul. He is only human and talking to someone, even for a few minutes now and then, can kill this feeling of abandonment, of being detached from society. He knows it's part of the lifestyle of being a writer, but it's the one part he could do without. Why can't his wife be a writer like him? They would sit here all day and face another and type away like there is no tomorrow.

By nine o'clock irritation gnaws at him like rats feasting on his flesh in the middle of night. Lucia is still not home, and she hasn't bothered calling again. He tried her mobile phone earlier on, but all he kept getting was her voice-mail—he doesn't want to leave another message because he's only going to repeat what he has previously said, and since she thinks of him as being irrational and short-fused, he doesn't want to make it worse for himself.

The yellow, plastic waste basket next to the kitchen table is filled with rumpled pieces of typing paper. The red ashtray is full to the brim. He spends more money on cigarettes and wine than on food, and at his age it's a disaster waiting to happen. He knows, but he's too depressed to even try to change his lifestyle. Maybe it's a form of slow suicide, he thinks, and if it's the case, the sooner, the better. Life is overrated, and the human race is a virus.

He stands up from his chair and paces nervously from one side of the kitchen to the other, cigarette in hand, his hair somewhat messy, a three-day growth covering his face like some Greek-English pop star from the eighties.

Then a noise from the foyer.

His mind registers what he's just heard—Lucia inserting the key into the lock and opening the door.

She walks into the kitchen, dressed in this morning's grey suit. Her white blouse is opened to the third button, and he can just see a bit of her bone-colour bra, and it causes him to feel anger rising like a raging storm in the distance. Why is she showing her breasts to the rest of the world? Well, almost.

Lucia holds a black briefcase in her right hand. She looks tired but satisfied all at once, like someone who has just come back from a two-hour session at the gymnasium.

Or screwing a young man all afternoon.

Nathan shifts from the bench he is leaning against and walks up to her before she has time reach the middle of the kitchen, somewhere between the hallway and the entrance of the kitchen.

He says, "I want you to leave this place."

Lucia—he can see it on her face, her tensed muscles, her dark eye expressing confusion and irritability simultaneously—is taken back.

"What are you talking about?" she says.

"I don't think we should be together anymore."

"Have you gone totally insane?"

"I want you to pack your stuff and leave tonight."

Lucia drops her briefcase to the floor. "And where the fuck am I supposed to go?"

There goes the f-word again.

"Why don't you ask that gigolo you've been fucking? I'm sure he'll be delighted to hear you got rid of me."

He is doing it too, the f-wording finally bringing himself down to her level.

Lucia walks up to him. She places both hands on his shoulders, like a mother does to a child who's been disobedient. "Listen to me, I'm not seeing anyone, okay?"

They stare at one another for a few seconds.

Then he says, "Then why aren't we fucking anymore?"

She removes her hands from his shoulders and shrugs. "Jerk-off if you're horny. We've been together twelve years. People don't fuck one another after twelve of being together."

"That's the biggest, bullshit excuse I've ever heard."

"I'm tired, I've been working all day, and I don't feel like fucking like rabbits."

Nathan pushes her with his right hand. "Just leave, okay?"

"I'm paying the rent here."

"The lease is under my name. Please leave now."

Lucia chews over his demand for a few seconds. "Fine, but you're making a mistake, it's not what you think."

"What is it then?" He sniffs the air, the acrid smell hitting his senses like a punch in the face. "You even smell like his cock!"

"You're such an arsehole!" She shrugs and leaves the kitchen.

He shakes his head in confusion and disgust.

It's for the best, he tries to convince himself.

CHAPTER TWO

Lucia walks along the hallway and enters another room, the bedroom where they made love every night of the week when they first moved in together. She doesn't turn the bedroom light on, but there is a glow from the street light outside, which makes the room bright enough for her to see what she is doing. She can see the bed, the mirror in the corner, the side-tables, a tallboy and a chair. The room feels too familiar, like an old pair of shoes, but she finds no comfort in familiarity. Routine bores her. Her senses are deadened when her sensory experiences are limited to routine. She doesn't believe people are meant to be doing the same thing day-in and day-out. She can't understand why you would want to make love to the same person for the rest of your life. She's seen it with her parents, day after day, night after night, looking at one another and eventually having nothing left to say. Even though she has passed the age of forty, she doesn't feel sexually dead just yet, and in another ten years, she will lose her looks, and then it would be next to impossible to get men to look at her.

She walks up to the wardrobe, opens it and removes a yellow cardboard box from the top shelf. She opens the box, shuffles through some papers. Old bills, car insurance, home contents insurance, health cover, tax return. She retrieves a small, silver bottle filled with Kentucky bourbon.

She looks towards the entrance of the bedroom to check if Nathan is coming after her.

He isn't. He's probably trying to figure out how he is going to pay the rent without a salary.

She unscrews the cap and takes a mouthful. The heat goes straight through her oesophagus and warms her lungs and stomach. The relief is instantaneous. She discovered what alcohol can do to you when she was in her late teens and had to be dragged away from a nightclub after falling asleep on the dance floor.

When done, she places the bottle back inside the box, and the box back on the top shelf of the wardrobe.

She sits on the bed and brings her hands to her face in despair. She loves this apartment—not the bedroom so much —and she knows cheating on Nathan is wrong, but she can't help herself. Sexual drive is stronger than willpower or common sense. Freud was right. Everything is sexual, even if some deny it.

But Nathan's friends are her friends, so whose side are they going to be on when they have to choose between the cheating whore and the innocent man?

Lucia looks straight into the camera. She is dressed in a blue, cotton blouse, and her hair is neatly styled. She knows the recording is not supposed to be for broadcast, but she doesn't want to take a chance, so this morning she put on her best semi-formal outfit. Her lipstick is cherry red and contrasts well against the blackness of her hair. The room smells of moisture and coffee and reminds her of her study days when she used to lock herself in a cubicle at the university library and memorise legal cases she had to be over-familiar with if she wanted to pass the bar. She was never good at critical thinking, but she found it easy to absorb and remember facts, dates and cases.

She straightens up on the green plastic chair and says, "Are you filming?"

"It's rolling," the interviewer says.

"Okay, well, he's dumped me. I came home the other night, and he kicked me out of the house."

"Were you having an affair?"

"Yes."

"But you told him you weren't?"

"He wouldn't have understood."

"Can you explain?"

"Okay, well, you know men and women are different. They don't think the same way, they're wired differently."

"Okay."

"Men think women are monogamists, or they want to believe they are. Men are polygamists, and they accept it. But they won't accept women are polygamists too."

"What about people who have been married for forty years?"

"They just haven't found anyone who wants to screw them, or they're very discreet, or they pretend they don't know what's going on, so they can keep the relationship going because of financial reasons, or because they've got kids."

"How old is this other man you're seeing?"

"He's twenty-one."

"And how old are you?"

"I'm forty-one."

"Doesn't the age difference bother you?"

"Love doesn't care about age."

"So, you're in love with this young man?"

"I'm in love with Lorenzo, yes, I think so."

"You don't care about what people think?"

"He doesn't have an issue with age. I don't have an issue with age." She takes a sip from her water. "Why is it okay for an older man to go out with a younger woman, but when an older woman goes out with a younger man, it's taboo? Who makes up those rules?"

"Do you think it's still taboo in this day and age? Older female celebrities always seem to be going out with younger men. It's more widely accepted now."

"I'm not a celebrity, so it's kind of different in the real world."

"Is this why you haven't married?"

"I don't believe in marriage, people get married just to get divorced."

"Tell me a little about Lorenzo."

She tells him everything he wants to know, the way she would tell a best friend the most intimate details of her sexual life. It almost turns her on, and she is surprised at how much she enjoys doing this, even though she doesn't really like the interviewer. Just the thought of Lorenzo churns her insides. The nakedness of his firm, young body lingers in her mind's eye a whole hour after the interview has ended.

Lucia and Lorenzo are sitting on a bench at the St Kilda Botanical Garden, right under an elm tree, their faces half-covered by shadows. The sky is blue and the air smells of flowers and freshly mowed lawn. Two young boys, eight and ten, dressed in yellow jerseys, are kicking a black-and-white, leather soccer ball back-and-forth; a middle-aged woman is walking a border collie in the distance; and a young couple dressed in jeans and matching white shirts are pushing a yellow, vinyl pram with red wheels. It's warm enough to not wear a coat or a jumper, but in less than an hour the temperature will drop by five degrees, and people in the park will be heading to the comfort of their homes.

Lorenzo is dressed casually in designer jeans and a dark blue, slim-fit tee-shirt, very young and hip looking. His coffee skin is flawless, his nose straight and his hair charcoal black. His big brown eyes are framed in long eyelashes and manicured eyebrows. He is a metro-sexual man of his generation, in touch with both his feminine and masculine sides in equal parts.

And it's one of the reasons Lucia choose to have an affair with him. She got a little tired of macho men who communicate with a ' yes' or a 'no' or a grunt. She needed someone who was still sensitive and not worn-out by the emotional tug-of-war of long-running relationships. She needed to feel she was still alive, she was still a woman, she still had what it took for men to be attracted to her.

And Lorenzo fulfilled those needs.

Lorenzo says, "I've never met anyone like you, you know?" and takes her hand into his. "What are we going to do about Nathan? He knows, doesn't he?"

"He knows, but he can't prove anything," Lucia says.

Lorenzo rests his head against Lucia's shoulder. "Do you think we're bad people?"

"Do *you* think we're bad people?"

"I don't know, maybe we are. Maybe I'm the evil toy boy who's destroying a marriage."

"Nathan and I are not married."

"Destroying a relationship, then."

"We don't even have that either. It's a relationship of convenience. We're not even good friends."

"Not a very nice thing to say."

"But it's true. People find themselves in these so-called relationships, and it's very intense for the first few years, and then it fizzles out."

"Do you think it's going to be the same with us?"

Lucia looks at Lorenzo adoringly. "Never."

They kiss.

Lorenzo says, "I want us to live together."

"Can't do."

"Why not?"

"What are your parents going to say?"

"They'll just have to accept it."

Lucia notices a white and pink ice cream van not far from where they are sitting and sees the opportunity to change the conversation. She doesn't like negotiating commitment and discussing future plans. She tried with Nathan, and it got her nowhere. Lorenzo is a fuck-fantasy, but he doesn't need to know. He's too young to understand the needs of a woman twice his age. It's best to let him bask in the belief of eternal love, the way young people do when they have yet to experience the burning fires of human deception, the consuming and unrelenting appetite of carnal obsession, the realisation of how true love is nothing but a fantasy imagined to keep society tamed and obedient. If they couldn't believe in eternal love at a young age, they would have no need to move on with life.

"Want an ice cream?" she asks.

"Okay."

They stand up from the bench and walk towards the ice cream van.

Lorenzo says, "So, you don't want to live with me?"

Lucia turns around to face him, and they stop walking. "You have no idea about how badly I want to live with you— but we have to be a bit patient. You look like you've just graduated from high school." She lies but it doesn't bother her.

"I thought you said our age difference didn't bother you?"

"It doesn't, but—"

"But what?"

"But people talk, and, you know, they have a tendency to be nasty."

"I don't care if you're older than me, it's sexy."

She takes off.

He follows and catches up with her.

"I don't want to use you," she says.

"Use me for what?"

"Take advantage of you."

They arrive at the ice cream van.

He says, "Hey, you're not twisting my arm here, I'm with you because I choose to be."

"Can we drop the subject?" she says. Now he is getting rather annoying, and she knows her tone might have been a little harsh.

"Okay, sure."

They order two vanilla soft serves and eat them in silence on the way back to the car.

Lucia and Lorenzo are lying in bed, a white sheet half covering their bodies, hot and sweaty, the room filled with a musky, adult smell. The bedroom is in Lorenzo's apartment and is very neat for a young man. The pine furniture is cheap but well looked after, and there are prints of unknown paintings on the walls.

They just made hot, passionate love, and he managed to bring her up to orgasm twice.

"Where are you going to stay now?" Lorenzo says, his firm body stretched to its full length.

"He can keep the apartment. At a friend's I guess."

"What friend?"

"You don't know her."

"What's her name?"

"Samantha."

"Okay."

Lorenzo gets up from the bed, totally naked. He goes to the chair in the bedroom and pulls on a pair of jeans, not bothering with the underwear.

Lucia is mesmerised by his toned-up body and smooth skin. "You're a handsome, young man, you know?" she says.

Lorenzo turns around. "So why don't you move in with me?

"Come here."

He looks at her.

19

She smiles. "Just come here."

He slowly walks to the bed. "What?"

She grabs his hands and pulls him on the bed.

He laughs and falls on the sheet.

She bends over and kisses him.

When they are done, she pulls back.

She says, "If you really want to move in with me, okay, I'll move in with you."

"Are you serious?"

"Dead serious."

"Really?"

"Promise."

He smiles and folds his hands together like a child. "Oh, this is so exciting." He wraps his arms around her neck. "I love you so much."

He kisses her.

There is no turning back now, she knows.

It's the evening, the end of the day for nine-to-five working people. Lucia and Samantha are at a table drinking at the local pub. There's soft middle-of-the-road rock playing in the background, and the whole place smells of beer and spirits. The walls are wood panel and the decor is glass and metal, giving it a modern look combined with classic design from a bygone era. A redhead is sitting alone at the bar nursing a spirit, and a couple of men in their mid-forties are having a chat over drinks at the end of the room.

A workman in blue jeans and white tee-shirt is fixing a light fitting near the entrance. It's not happy hour yet, but soon the place will be crowded with people who want to unwind after work but are not ready to go home just yet.

Lucia is drinking a light beer and Samantha a rum-and-cola. They are dressed casually but neatly. Samantha wears a green dress and Lucia black trousers and a yellow blouse.

"He knows," Lucia. She tells Samantha everything, and she

doesn't even feel guilty about it. Men are certain they know how women think, but they don't and never will.

Samantha sips from her drink, the ice cubes clicking against the glass. "Did you tell him?"

"I told him he was being paranoid, but he knows. Thanks for trying, anyway."

"I was meant to talk to him first, but he kicked you out before I had a chance."

"It's doesn't matter, anyway, it's better this way."

Samantha locks eyes with Lucia. "How's Lorenzo?"

Lucia smiles. "Very nice, you know what young men are like."

"No, I mean, *how* is he?"

"He's good. We're going away this weekend, we're going to move in together." Lucia drinks from her glass and smiles.

"Really?"

"He insisted. I was reluctant, but he's right. I'm only reluctant because of what people might think."

"Fuck people."

"Yeah, it's what he said."

"I mean what business is it to everyone else what you do with your life? It's your life after all."

"Tell me about it."

CHAPTER THREE

Lorenzo is looking at the camera the way someone looks at a person when they are having a conversation. He is dressed with a black shirt, his hair perfectly combed and his skin glowing .

The interviewer leans slightly forward and says, "And the fact she's twice your age doesn't bother you?"

"No, not at all. In fact, it's the other way around.'

"You find her attractive?"

"Very attractive. You know, girls my age have no experience, and all they want is someone to pay for everything. Given the choice..."

"Okay, but what happens when she's sixty and you're forty?"

"What do you mean *what happens*?"

"Are you still going to be with her?"

"I love her, so yes, of course I'm going to be with her."

"Are you seeing anyone else?"

Lorenzo pauses, seemingly confused by the question. "A woman? Or a man?"

"A woman? Yeah, sure, a man or a woman."

"Yes, but it's not really serious, it's just for fun. Like a buddy thing."

"Can you tell us about him?"

"We went to school together, and we've never stopped being friends since then, sometimes a little more than friends."

"More than friends?"

"He was the first person I kissed."

"Really? How old were you?"

"Fourteen. We were just experimenting. We wanted to teach ourselves how to kiss properly, you know just in case we found ourselves with a girl, and we wanted to know how to do it."

"And what happened?"

"He was the first person I made love to."

"How old were you then?"

"Sixteen or seventeen, I can't remember exactly. We were still at school."

"When you say you made love to him, you mean you had sex with him?"

Lorenzo looks puzzled. "You want me to give you details?"

"If you want to, you don't have to, it's up to you."

"I don't mind."

Lorenzo thinks this over. "You're not going to show this video to anyone, are you?"

"No, it's only for research."

"It was really nice, it wasn't really about the sex, okay, it was a bit about the sex too, but it was more about having someone you could be really close to, someone who loved you for who you were, who didn't ask you to change all the time. We understood each other completely, and I've never had this level of intimacy with girls back then. I was never really good with girls my own age, I'm still not."

"Okay, I understand. Are you still seeing this boy?"

"Yes, I still see Tom, it's hard not to."

Lorenzo is sitting on his bed at home with Tom, another young man, early twenties and attractive, blonde hair and powdered skin. Tom's ears are pierced with slippers. He wears a little too much lip gloss, and it looks as if he is in fact wearing a pale shade of lipstick. His blue eyes sparkle with excitement and happiness.

They move and lock their fingers together and kiss.

They make love fast and energetically, as if time is running out, and they'll never get another chance again.

When done, Lorenzo gets off the bed and dresses with his jeans and blue tee-shirt.

Tom stays in bed, pleased with himself. "It was great. Was it good for you too?" he says.

Lorenzo doesn't reply.

Tom has a concerned look on his face. "You have to think about it?"

Lorenzo turns around to face him. "We need to talk."

"Oh, like that, is it?"

"I'm seeing someone else."

There is awkward silence in the room for about five seconds.

Tom shifts on the bed. "What's his name?"

"He is a *she*. Her name is Lucia. She's Italian."

"Oh!"

Tom gets up from the bed and gets dressed. "How did it happen?"

"We work together. I've known her since I began working for the law firm. She's really nice."

"How old is she?"

"Forty-one, but she's really nice." Lorenzo turns around and faces Tom. "I'm so in love, I've never been in love like this before."

Tom smiles at Lorenzo. He walks up to him and wraps his arms around his waist. "If you're happy, then I'm happy for you."

"Thanks."

They kiss.

They pull back.

Tom continues to get dressed, clearly upset.

Lorenzo fixes his hair in front of the mirror.

Tom says, "So why can't we see each other anymore?"

"I didn't say we can't see each other, but just as friends. I don't want to be confused about my sex life. I want to keep everything straight."

"I see."

"I don't want to lie to her."

Ten minutes later Tom and Lorenzo are sitting opposite one

24

another and are having coffee and toast. The balcony windows are opened, and there is traffic noise in the distance.

Tom says, "Is Lucia married?"

"It's over. Her partner dumped her a couple of days ago."

"They've got kids?"

"No."

"It's not too bad then." He takes a bite from his butter-and-jam toast. "Aren't you worried she's too old for you?"

"No. I don't think she's too old. It seems like everyone else thinks it's an issue."

"These types of May-December relationships never work. She always ends up going back to the husband, or the wife if it's the other way around."

Lorenzo takes a mouthful of coffee. "She won't. This time it's the real thing, we both know it."

Tom smiles, but it's a smile implying Lorenzo is naive, and Lorenzo sees this but ignores it at first. He picks up his empty coffee mug and stands from his chair.

"I know what you're thinking," Lorenzo says.

"I didn't say anything."

"You're giving me that look again."

"What look?"

Lorenzo walks up the kitchen bench and smashes the cup in the sink. "Why does everyone keep on telling me what to do?" He's cut his hand with the cup. It's bleeding.

Tom can see the blood from where he is sitting. "Oh, Christ, let me take a look." He stands from his chair and walks up to where Lorenzo is. He examines the cut on Lorenzo's hand.

Lorenzo says, "Why can't people just leave me alone? It's my choice in life to decide who I want to be with."

"I'm sorry, I didn't mean to upset you."

Tom takes the dish cloth from the kitchen bench and wipes the blood from Lorenzo's hand. "I just don't want her to break your heart."

"I love her, Tom, okay?"

"I understand, and I'm sorry if I've made you upset. If it's what you want, then be with her."

"I don't understand what love has to do with age? People are incredibly self-centred and insensitive to other people's feelings. I would never tell another person to not go out with someone if they are in love."

Tom moves forward and gives him a hug.

"Don't worry about it," he says. "I'm on your side."

CHAPTER FOUR

Tom's bedroom looks like a teenager's room, even though he is in his early twenties. There are posters of pop stars on the walls, and a small study desk. He is one from this generation where moving on with life doesn't make much sense if you haven't figured out what you want yet.

He is sitting on the edge of his bed, thinking about Lorenzo, thinking about his life, thinking about how everything keeps on fucking up around him and wishing he were someone else.

He opens a drawer by the side table and removes a small mirror, a small bag filled with coke and a short straw. He does lines on the mirror and takes the drug in through his nostril.

After he's done, he falls back on the bed and stares at a photo of Lorenzo.

The door of his bedroom opens without warning.

Tom's father walks in. He has red neck written all over his face, his head shaved like an ex-con, his tattoos on display like a pimp. "Weren't you supposed to start work at ten?"

Tom looks towards the door. "Not going."

"Why not?"

"Don't feel like it."

"What are you talking about?"

"In fact, I'm not going anymore. I don't like this job."

Tom's Father walks up to the bed. "Are you stoned again?"

Tom just stares at him. "Fuck off, will you?"

"I've had it with your shit. You live here, you don't pay rent, you don't buy food, you sit around all day doing nothing, you get high and you never help around. I think it's time for you to move out."

"Yeah, whatever you reckon."

"I'm serious. I want you out of this house by tonight."

"And where the fuck am I supposed to go?"

"Your problem. Pack you shit and get out of this house. You need to learn to be responsible, and you're never going to be responsible as long as you live in this house."

Tom's Father leaves the room and shuts the door.

Tom grabs the clock radio from the side table and throws it against the door.

"Fuck you, you piece of shit!"

The sound of the clock crashing is deafening.

Tom is walking past boutiques by himself. He's just done his hair and looks good in his black, leather jacket. The sky is blue and the air is warm. He enters a bar, all mirrors and metal, the modern version of the pub. He walks up to Walter, the barman, mid-thirties, overweight, sad blue Coker-Spaniel eyes.

"I need a place to stay for a few days," Tom says.

Walter looks at him. "What will you have?"

"Short black." He waits a few seconds, then: "I'm serious, I need a place to crash for a few days."

Walter makes the coffee. "I heard you. Why are you asking me?"

"Because you've got a house with three bedrooms, and you're the only one who lives in it."

"We have this discussion every couple of months."

"This time it's urgent, I'm *serious*."

Walter brings the coffee to the bar top. "I know you're serious."

"Come on, it's just for a week at the most. My father's just kicked me out of home, and I've got nowhere else to stay."

Walter stares at him. "One week?"

"One week max, guaranteed. I'm starting to look for a new place tomorrow."

Walter sighs. "Okay, one week only, and I'm not kidding, one week from now, I'm throwing all your stuff into the streets."

"Thank you so much, I owe you one."

"Yeah, sure..."

Tom sips from his short black. "Lorenzo broke up with me."

Walter's eyes light up. "Really?"

"Yesterday."

"What happened?"

"Found someone else. A *woman*."

"Really?"

"Yeah, and he tells me he is in love with her after he fucks me. Typical."

Walter looks a little concerned. "Is this why you want to move in with me? I told you it was over. I'm not going back on my word. I'm not gay, it was a mistake. I was confused, I've just broken up with Marilyn, I had no idea what I was doing."

"I'm not asking for sex here, just a roof, honest."

Walter looks at him suspiciously. "As long as we've got this straight from the start."

"Cross my heart, there's no hidden agenda here."

Walter points his finger at Tom's face. "Don't fuck with me. It's the first time in a long time I feel good about myself since my life turned to shit."

"You're such a drama queen."

"I'm serious."

"I know you are, and that's what worries me."

Tom is facing the camera. He looks tired, as if he has not slept for a week. His eyelids are heavy and his lips are colourless and dry. "Everyone always leaves me. I don't under-stand."

"Are you saying you're incapable of staying in a relationship and it's your fault?" the interviewer says.

"It's what it feels like. First there was Walter, and then Lorenzo, and I don't understand why they are all turning their backs on who they really are."

"What do you mean?"

"You don't just stop being gay overnight. Either you are or you're not. I wouldn't sleep with a woman just because it's what the world expects of me."

"What if they're telling the truth?"

"No way."

"Okay then, would you accept they might be bi-sexual?"

Tom looks thoughtful. He takes a sip from a glass of water on the table. "I guess it's a possibility, but why do I always end up in bed with bi-sexual men?"

"It might be nothing more than a coincidence."

Tom takes another sip from his glass. "Can we talk about something else? This is getting me depressed."

"Okay, what do you want to talk about?"

"I don't know." He thinks for a few seconds. "What's this for again?"

"Research."

"Research for what?"

"Relationships."

"Does it have to be sexual relationships?

"No necessarily. Any type of relationship."

"Can I talk about my father?"

"If you want."

"Actually, it's depressing too." Tom pauses for a few seconds and thinks. "He's a prick. He doesn't know I'm gay, and I'll never be able to tell him because he'll end up killing me."

"Are you sure?"

"You don't know my father, he's a total arsehole. Doesn't

care about anyone but himself, which is why my mother left us."

Tom's mother, Tom's father and Tom are at the dinner table.

Tom's Mother looks frail and mortified. She is slim with dark hair and dark eyes and china-white complexion.

Tom's father takes a bite from his food.

He looks up to his wife. "This tastes like shit. I work all day to come home to cooking that tastes like shit."

"I'm sorry."

"I bet you are. What do you do all day? You only have to look after the house and cook one meal a day? And you can't even do that right!"

Tom looks annoyed but says nothing. It's the nightly ritual of abuse and defence.

"I had a headache, I wasn't feeling well," she says.

"Then take a headache tablet." Tom's father bangs the table with his fist. "Jesus Christ! It's not as if I'm asking for a miracle here!"

Tom looks up. "Just leave her alone."

"What did you say?"

"Just leave her alone. She didn't do anything."

"Oh, yeah? At least we agree, she never does anything." He thinks for a few seconds. "And don't talk to me that way. Show some respect."

"Maybe you should show some respect instead of treating everyone like shit."

Tom's Father stands from his chair and tries to grab Tom by the shirt. "Respect? I'll teach you some fuckin' respect."

Tom stands from his chair.

Tom's Father stands right in front of him. "You ever talk to me like that again, and I'll smash your face in."

Tom says nothing and just stares point blank.

"And don't eye-ball me, son. Go to your room."

Tom stares a little longer.

"I'm warning you."

Tom looks at his mother.

She nods.

Tom leaves the table and then the room.

"Fuckin' son of yours. I swear he obviously takes it from you."

Tom's Mother says nothing.

"One of these days..."

Tom is in bed, the sheet down halfway, his chest exposed. There's movement next to him.

"How did you sleep?" Tom asks.

"Good," Walter says.

Walter turns around and looks at Tom straight on, holding eye contact. "When I said you had to leave by the end of the week, well, you don't really have to. You can stay if you want."

Tom thinks this over and seems to be evaluating his surroundings. "I'll find a place by the end of the week. It's okay."

"No, I mean you don't have to, you can stay here if you want."

Tom scratches his head. "Oh, okay, yeah, sure, if you want me to."

"I want you to."

Walter turns around and kisses Tom. He pulls back and says, "I don't like living by myself. I thought I did, but now you're here, well, I realise I really don't like living by myself."

"Then I'll stay."

They kiss and make love.

Walter penetrates Tom, and it's obvious Tom is not really enjoying it. Walter is overweight and it makes the sex uncomfortable.

Walter groans and moans, and when he's done, he pulls back and smiles.

Tom smiles back and pretends to be happy. At least he

doesn't have to worry about food and shelter for a while longer, as long as he can put up with the sex. He's not going to walk straight for two days, but it's all part of the game.

There's nothing free in this world.

CHAPTER FIVE

Walter is in bed with Marilyn. They just finished having sex. Marilyn has dishwater, blonde hair, big breasts and sad, blue eyes. There's a bit of weight on her, and she would look almost fantastic if she dropped twenty kilos or so.

Marilyn says, "I needed that so much."

They both stand from the bed, totally naked.

Marilyn begins to dress, putting on her red panties first. "I'm sorry to have bothered you, but I haven't had a fuck in two weeks, and I was getting desperate."

"It's okay, you don't have to explain," Walter says.

"I could have picked up some strange man at a bar, but it's too complicated. I don't want to get back into a relationship. I'm not ready yet. And I know you're a good fuck, at least it was something I could always count on."

"Thanks," he says with no emotion or feelings in his voice. This sex thing with Marilyn is just routine, not something he truly enjoys. He hasn't cared about women for a long time, but he's kept his mixed emotions deep inside for too long.

Marilyn finishes pulling up her jeans and buttons up her green blouse. "How long is Tom staying with you?"

"As long as he wants."

"Are you fucking him?"

Walter gives her a stare like throwing knifes. "It's none of your business."

"I don't want to catch a disease or something."

"He's not positive, okay, and neither am I."

"Jeez, you're a little touchy, aren't you? If you didn't want me to come over, you should have said so."

"Don't start, Marilyn, not everything I do is about you."

Ten minutes later, they are in the kitchen having a breakfast of coffee and toast. It's Walter's apartment, totally clean, the way you would expect an apartment of a gay man to be.

Marilyn says, "Why did we ever break up?"

"Love doesn't last forever," Walter replies.

"Who says?"

"It's a fact of life."

"I'm wondering if we did the right thing?"

"In what way?"

"In separating."

"You left me, Marilyn."

"You cheated on me. With a *man*!"

Walter takes a bite from his toast. "I know, it's my fault."

"I think it was better when we were together. Maybe I should come back. What do you think?"

Walter gives her a long stare. "It wouldn't work."

"Why not?"

"You know why."

"I don't care if you fuck Tom. I can live with it as long as you continue to fuck me too."

Walter drinks from his coffee mug. "Do we have to have this conversation now?"

"When else are we going to have it? We don't live together anymore. When are we supposed to talk?"

"We don't need to talk, Marilyn. We're no longer in a relationship."

Marilyn seems hurt. She drops her toast on the plate. "Fine, if it's the way you want it."

"It's over, we agreed it was over."

"I'm not coping, okay. It's hard financially, it's hard

emotionally, I don't know if it's what I want."

Walter finishes his coffee. "I have to go to work. Just lock the door properly when you leave."

He walks up to the sink and tosses his breakfast dishes in the grey water. He aims for the exit of the kitchen. He turns to Marilyn. "I'm sorry it didn't work out, but you can't get back love once it's gone."

"Not true. I'm still in love with you."

"No, you're not. You just miss the life we used to have."

He steps out of the kitchen and disappears into the hallway.

Marilyn yells, "Did you know it was my birthday today?"

"Happy birthday," he calls back, no caring or emotion in his tone.

He slams the front door of the apartment.

Marilyn stares at her coffee.

Fuck!

Marilyn and Lucia are sitting at a table with a drink. The coffee shop is virtually empty so early in the afternoon. It's sunny outside, and most people are either at work or enjoying the outdoors. There's a strong smell of coffee and sweet cream cakes coming from the bar section of the cafe. It's a nice, little place for friends to catch up on gossip.

"I don't understand them," Marilyn says. Her eyes are heavy from crying and not sleeping enough. Her blonde hair is messed up. She wears a red cardigan, which makes her look older than she actually is. "I know it's sounds like a cliché, but why does it have to be so difficult? We are all made of flesh and bone after all."

Lucia takes a sip from her coffee and places the cup down on a white saucer. "Men don't even understand themselves, so it's unlikely you're going to figure them out."

"I'm offering him unconditional love. He can even have his boyfriend if he wants to, but he won't have me back. Do you have any idea how much this hurts?"

Lucia takes another sip from her coffee. "You need to find someone else. Do what I've done. Find someone younger."

"I don't really like younger men. They're so insecure all the time, it's like baby-sitting."

"Why don't I set you up with Lorenzo for one night? It will do you good."

Marilyn looks at Lucia, surprised. "Are you crazy?"

"I'm serious, I don't mind sharing him. I think he'll find you attractive."

Marilyn giggles. "You're not serious?"

"You want to?"

"I don't think so."

"You don't know what you're missing out. He will make you forget about Walter."

Marilyn goes red. "It's totally immoral."

"Yes, it's immoral, but he will make you feel like a real woman again."

Lucia takes Marilyn's hand into hers. "It's your birthday gift, let me do this for you."

The waiter walks up to them. He is short, late twenties, Italian-looking with black-rimmed glasses and clean, white shirt. It's the same waiter who served Samantha and Nathan the other day.

The girls laugh at the same time.

The waiter says, "Is everything okay?" He seems a little offended, as if they were making fun of him.

Lucia says, "Oh, yes, sorry, it's just a private joke."

"Very well." He leaves them, looking sideways to check if they are not laughing about him again.

"What about him? He's kind of cute," Lucia says.

"I don't think so," Marilyn says. She thinks for a few seconds. "I'll have Lorenzo."

"Good on you."

They both giggle like a couple of teenage girls.

That same night Marilyn has sex with Lorenzo at his apartment. He has a good body on him, and she now understands why Lucia is attracted to him. He smells good too, a little overdone with the aftershave, but it's better than the smell of armpits and sweaty balls. There's something incredibly delicious about him, but she can't figure what exactly. Maybe it's just the combination that works perfectly.

Lorenzo takes Marilyn from behind, both his hands on her wide butt cheeks, spreads them generously so he can enter her with ease. Her cunt is moist and filled like a sponge, and it makes the whole thing bearable.

Between Tom, Lucia and Marilyn, he is starting to feel like a sex machine, and he's not sure he really likes it.

Marilyn is facing the camera. She looks happy for a change. Her blonde hair is groomed. She wears a yellow blouse and gold crucifix.

"It's was great," she says. "I never thought it would be this great."

The interviewer says, "Do you think it will help you to forget Walter?"

"I think it will. You know, it's strange, but I didn't think it would, but it has. But don't tell him."

"I wouldn't discuss with Walter anything you discuss with me."

Marilyn takes a sip from her water and then says, "Do you think it's all there is to it?"

"I'm sorry?" The interviewer doesn't follow her train of thought.

"Love. Do you think it's all there is to love? Why do I feel so relieved just because I had sex with someone other than Walter?"

"I don't know. Maybe you've just found out you don't have to depend on the one person to make you happy."

"You think so?"

"I'm not sure. What do you think?"

"You might be right. It's kind of true I guess. When I left Walter, I felt as if my whole life was over. But last night with Lorenzo, it's just put things into a new perspective."

She takes another sip from her water on the table.

"Are you happy?" the interviewer asks.

"Happier than I've been in a long time. Lucia was right, and I thought she was just being stupid, but she was right."

"Do you feel the need to go back to Walter? Will you go back to Walter?"

"To be his fuck buddy? I don't think so. I think it's time for me to look for someone else."

"How?"

"I don't know, but it's fairly easy for a woman to get a man into bed. Most men are desperate for sex."

"Really?"

"It's a fact. Give them half a chance, and they'll fuck the first attractive woman who gives them the opportunity."

"And knowing this fact, do you still think finding another man is going to make you happy?"

"You can't rely on one single person to ensure your happiness. I've learned my lesson. I feel like a new person. It's as if I've just been re-born. I don't think I'm ever going to miss him again. It's strange, isn't it? Just one night with a stranger can change your life entirely."

"So you think you're going to be all right now?"

"Absolutely, never felt so good in my life."

She smiles widely at the camera, as if to prove a point.

That same night Marilyn is sitting on the edge of her bed in her studio apartment. She looks a little shocked. She holds a picture of Walter and herself on her lap.

They both look happy, smiling in unison.

She stares at the picture for a few seconds and then she hugs the picture.

Suddenly she trembles and begins to cry. Memories coming flooding back, and the pain is just unbearable. Those who have not had a broken heart would never understand how incredibly painful it can be.

She opens a drawer by the wooden side table and removes a handgun, a Raven P25 25ACP in Chrome. It's cold to the touch. She unlocks the security latch and checks it's loaded.

She puts the guns in her mouth, the taste of metal on her tongue.

It's all going to be over soon.

She let the tears stream down her face and squeezes the trigger.

The pain vanishes instantaneously.

CHAPTER SIX

Nathan is facing the camera. He looks tired, as if he hasn't slept for a couple of days. His hair is ruffled and his white shirt is open down to the third button, exposing some of his chest hair. He has taken up smoking again in the studio, even though the interviewer has told him it was best if he refrained from smoking.

Nathan says, "I didn't really know Marilyn well. She was Lucia's friend. She came to dinner a few times, and I always thought she was really confident. It's kind of a shock she took her own life."

"How do you think Walter is taking it?" the interviewer asks.

"He hasn't said much. Not to me anyway."

"What about Lucia?"

"She took it pretty badly, keeps telling us it's her fault, it was her gun. She lent it to Marilyn because Marilyn was staying on her own, and she thought she could do with the extra protection."

"Lucia has a gun?"

"I bought it for her birthday two years ago. I didn't like her coming home late at night without protection."

"What happened to the gun?"

"Lucia found Marilyn's body. She took the gun and called the police from a phone booth."

"Does this mean you and Lucia are going to stay together?"

"I don't think so, she's made up her mind about what she wants."

"So there's no chance whatsoever."

"None."

Nathan squashes the last of the cigarette in the ashtray on the table next to his chair.

Two days later Nathan and Lucia are making love like animals. First he takes her from behind and grabs her hair and pulls it back. She seems to be enjoying it, or at least she's doing a good job at looking as if she's enjoying.

He cups her breasts while he pushes his erection deep inside her. It feels fantastic with-out a condom, which he hates wearing. His sweat is dripping all over her back. He likes how she doesn't shave because nothing turns him on more than a woman with a wild bush.

He explodes inside her, his groaning louder now.

When they're done, they fall back on the bed.

Nathan catches his breath.

Lucia says, "I'm sorry I was such a bitch." She wipes herself between the legs with a towel she left by the side table.

Nathan doesn't reply.

She adds, "I won't see him again if you don't want me to."

He turns to face her. "It's not about what I want, it's about what you want."

"I want to stay with you," she says.

"Is it because Marilyn is dead, and you're a little confused?"

"It's because I've made a mistake."

Nathan chews over her comment for a few seconds. "Maybe it's best if we stay apart for a little while," he finally says, "you know just so you give yourself the chance to think clearly."

Lucia is about to say something, but she doesn't.

Instead she steps off the bed naked and puts on white

underwear and a yellow dress.

Nathan looks at her.

He says, "You're going back to work on Monday?"

"Yes."

"You should take some time off."

"I don't want to."

"You should really."

She turns to face him. "I think I'm capable of assessing whether I am ready to go back to work or not."

They stay silence for half a minute.

"It was only a suggestion," Nathan says. "You're right, do what you want. You've never done otherwise anyway."

"What?"

"You know what I'm talking about."

She turns to the mirror and fixes her hair. "I don't want to argue with you, okay? I just want us to be friends again."

Nathan steps off the bed and walks to where Lucia is standing. He moves behind her, his arms around her waist.

He says, "I want to be your friend, but there's only so much a friend can take."

She turns around to face him. "Let me move back in with you, it's what I really want."

They are face-to-face, noses almost touching.

"Oh, Lucia, you're making everything so difficult."

She moves her head forward and kisses him. "Please."

"Can I think about it?"

"What is there to think about? Either you want me back, or you don't."

Nathan pulls back.

Lucia turns around and tries to hold his stare.

Nathan says, "Come on Sunday."

"Does this mean yes?"

"It means we might as well give it another chance. But things are going to have to change."

"Of course, I understand."

Lucia turns back to her reflection in the mirror and fixes her hair. She smiles to herself.

Men are idiots.

The ball is in her court again.

CHAPTER SEVEN

Lucia and Samantha are having a coffee at their local cafe. It's early afternoon, and as usual, there are not many people right after lunch. Elevator jazz is playing through the black, wall-mounted speakers, and the room smells of salt-water because of the open French windows.

Lucia removes a little, silver flask from her black handbag and pours some of the contents into her coffee. She stirs it as if it were perfectly normal.

"You're still drinking?" Samantha says.

"It's just to help me get by."

"You know, I don't want to preach here, but it's what all alcoholics say."

"I'm not an alcoholic."

"No, but you're going to become one if you don't watch yourself."

Lucia sips from her coffee and smiles. "Tastes *so* good."

There is an awkward silence.

"I'm worried about you," Samantha says.

"Because of the drinking?"

"Yes."

"You don't believe me when I say I'm not an alcoholic?"

"Lucia, how many people do you know carry a flask of alcohol in their handbags?"

Lucia stares at Samantha for a few seconds, and then:

"Okay, fine, you win."

She removes the flask from her handbag and hands it over the table to Samantha.

Samantha smiles. She puts the flask in her own bag. "Thank you."

More silence.

"You really want to move back with Nathan?" Samantha says.

"I told him so."

"You meant it?"

"Of course I mean it."

Lucia empties her coffee cup in one go.

The next morning Lucia faces the camera. She looks wide awake, but a little tense. The business attire is gone, and she is wearing jeans, a white shirt and a red cardigan.

The interviewer says, "But you have no intention of leaving Lorenzo?"

"I do, but we're still going to see one another now and then."

"And Nathan knows about this?"

"He thinks it's over between me and Lorenzo."

"You've told him?"

"Yes."

"You've lied to him, and it doesn't bother you?"

"It bothers me, yes, but I'm not perfect, and the world is not perfect, and life and emotions are always more complex than we think."

"Do you actually believe this, or you're just convincing yourself about what you've just said because it makes it easier for you to accept your infidelity?"

Lucia thinks over this for a few seconds. "Does it matter?"

"You don't think it matters?"

"Not really. It's all theory what you're saying here. Action is the only thing that matters. The reason why I'm doing what

I'm doing is irrelevant. It's whether I'm doing it or not that's really the issue."

"Okay." He adjusts the manual zoom of the camera lens. "And how's Lorenzo taking it?"

"He understands."

"Really?"

Lorenzo is having a short black by himself. It's late afternoon, and outside the sun is fading on the horizon. There are a few people in the shop, some having coffee and cake, others an early dinner.

The Italian waiter with the dark-framed glasses walks up to him. "Would you like some chocolate mud cake, sir?"

"No thanks, I'm waiting for someone."

"Very well, sir."

The waiter leaves.

Just then, Lucia comes up to the table. She's dressed in her work clothes—pressed, black skirt and matching jacket. Her hair is a little messy from having rushed from work. She fixes it with her right hand. "Sorry I'm late."

Lorenzo looks at his watch. "Half an hour late. I thought you were going to stand me up."

She kisses him on the lips and sits at the table. "A client who wouldn't leave. I couldn't exactly kick him out. He pays well, and he pays on time."

Lorenzo takes a sip from his coffee. "You want something to drink?"

"No, I'm okay, I can't stay long. I have another appointment at seven o'clock."

Lorenzo seems disappointed. "What is it you wanted to see me about?"

"We need to talk."

"I figured out that much."

Lucia seems a little scared. She takes his hand from across the table. "Don't take this the wrong way, but I can't move in

47

with you."

Lorenzo is stunned for a few seconds. He just stares at her for a moment and then says, "Why not?"

"I'm moving back with Nathan."

Lorenzo pulls back his hand. "Fuck!"

The people at the other tables look at them.

Lucia says, "I'm sorry."

"Tom was right. He said you would end up going back to your husband."

"I'm not married to him, and it's not what you think. I still want us to see one another."

Lorenzo finishes his short black. "What are you saying?"

"I'm saying it's not because I'm moving back with Nathan that I don't want to see you anymore."

Lorenzo stares at her, anger in his eyes. "You're saying you want to fuck him, and you want to fuck me too whenever it suits you?"

"Don't be like angry."

"What else do you want me to say? I'm over the moon? For fuck's sake, Lucia!"

The people at the other tables look at Lucia and Lorenzo again. They are clearly shocked by the language Lorenzo is using in public.

Lorenzo turns to them. "Mind your own fuckin' business."

The people turn around, embarrassed by Lorenzo's display of anger. They stare at their food and whisper to one another.

Lucia says, "It's really complex. I still feel for Nathan, especially after Marilyn's death."

"You're unbelievable, you know?" Lorenzo says.

"I'm sorry. I don't mean to be difficult. Maybe it won't work out with Nathan anyway."

"And then what?"

"And then if it doesn't work out, maybe we can move in together."

Lorenzo seems more relaxed. "You could have told me on

the phone."

"I didn't want to. I thought it would be better to tell you in person." She takes his hand again from across the table. He lets her do it. "I still think you're the sexiest man on the planet."

Lorenzo smiles and squeezes her hand. "You know I'm crazy about you. You know how difficult this is for me?"

"I know, and I'm sorry. I'll make it up to you." She stands from her chair. "Promise." She checks her watch. "I have to go now."

She circles the table to where Lorenzo is sitting and kisses him on the lips. "I'll call you tonight."

"Sure," he says.

She leaves and he is sitting alone by himself.

The waiter walks past him again.

" Excuse me," Lorenzo says.

The waiter stops at the table. "Yes?"

"I'll have some chocolate mud cake after all."

"Very well, sir."

CHAPTER EIGHT

Lorenzo is facing the camera. He looks tired and upset. He is drinking from a can of cola.

He says, "She made me believe she loved me."

"And now you think she doesn't?" the interviewer says.

"How can she if she's going back to Nathan?"

"Maybe she's confused after Marilyn took her own life."

Lorenzo takes another sip from his soda. "Okay, maybe she is, and maybe she isn't. She should be able to figure out what she wants. She asked me to fuck Marilyn. How do you think it makes me feel?"

"Is this why you've decided to sleep with Tom again?"

"I don't see why I should be faithful to Lucia only when she's moved back with Nathan. I tried to do the right thing by telling Tom it was over, but it's not fair she's moved back with her husband."

"Does it make you angry?"

"About her having gone back to him?"

"Yes."

"I would be a liar if I didn't admit I am somewhat angry. It doesn't mean that I hate her. It just means I have to think about myself, you can't trust anyone."

"You think so?"

"I trusted her one hundred percent. I believed every word she said. And Tom was right. She did end up going back to her husband."

"So, are you sleeping with Tom again? Is it some sort of revenge?"

"I don't know, and I don't really care. Everyone is looking out for themselves. Why shouldn't I?"

"Does this mean you're not in love with Lucia anymore?"

"You know what? Maybe I wasn't really in love with her in the first place, maybe it was just lust. Something different."

"I'm sure she wouldn't be happy to hear you talk this way."

"And I'm not happy she's moved back with Nathan, but it's life, isn't it?"

Tom turns to Lorenzo, who is still lying on the bed. They have just finished making love. The room smells of sex and maleness, and the morning sun gives it an amber glow. Lorenzo wonders why he keeps on doing this, giving in to everyone who wants to sleep with him, and yet receiving little in return.

Tom says,"Do you want me to get you anything from the shop?"

"I'm okay," Lorenzo says. "I have to meet my parents soon." He doesn't have to, but he wants to be alone for a while and prioritise what's important to him.

"I better get going too. Walter expected me one hour ago."

"How long are you going to stay at his place?"

Tom fixes his hair in front of a mirror. With his finger he spikes them up in places to give it a more edgy, youthful look. "I'm not in a rush to leave. Free rent, free food."

"He doesn't charge you for anything?"

Tom grins and looks at Lorenzo through the mirror. "Nope. Sponging at its best."

"It's not a very nice attitude. He's helping you here."

"I'm only kidding. Of course I appreciate what Walter is doing, but he always thinks there's more to sex than sex. I know he's going to fall in love with me all over again."

Lorenzo falls back on the bed. He knows Tom is lying and

is using Walter. Everyone seems to be using everyone else for their own gratification or needs.

"Why does love have to be so complicated?" he says.

Tom turns around and looks at Lorenzo. "Love is not complicated. People make it complicated."

Lorenzo looks at him. "You really think so?"

"Yes, absolutely."

"I don't know. I don't seem to know anyone in a relationship who doesn't have a problem with their partner. It's as if *everyone* is incapable of handling love."

Tom walks towards the bed. "Jeez, you're very philosophical this morning. What's going on with you?"

He sits on the edge of the bed and takes Lorenzo's hand.

Lorenzo smiles. "I don't know. I'm just a little tired of everything. It's feels as I am wasting too much time worrying about relationships instead of just finding something useful to do with my life."

Tom pulls his hand back. "Don't we all."

CHAPTER NINE

Walter and Tom are sitting on a bench opposite Williamstown beach. The sky is blue and the air warm, but it's a little too windy for people to enjoy a swim.

Walter says, "Marilyn freaked out when she knew you moved back to my place." He hasn't come around since his ex-wife has killed herself, and no matter what he thinks, there seems to be no way to get himself back on track. He hasn't eaten for most of the week, and just the idea of having sex with someone else makes him want to gag.

Tom doesn't answer immediately. There is an uncomfortable silence between them.

"It's doesn't mean it's your fault she killed herself," Tom finally says.

"She wanted us to repair our relationship. She still loved me, and I was cruel to her."

"You didn't put a gun to her head."

"Maybe if I'd agreed to give her a chance, she'd still be alive."

"It would have happened eventually. She was wired to take her own life."

Walter gives Tom a side-long glance. Anger is building up inside of him. Youth can be so ruthless, but he chooses to bite his tongue.

Tom says, "All I'm saying is for some people, it doesn't take much for them to flick off the switch."

"Marilyn was not suicidal. She never talked about killing herself."

"But she did kill herself. And just because she didn't talk about it, it doesn't mean she wasn't thinking about it."

They stare at the ocean opposite the park for a minute. A woman and a man are walking hand-in-hand, a brown Coker Spaniel by their side. They seem happy, as if all the troubles in the world are of no concern to them.

Walter know it could have been the same with Marilyn if only he'd kept his dick in his pants and chose not to sleep with other men. They could have been a happy couple too. She had never done anything wrong to him, and yet he pushed her away as if she was the one who was the problem in the first place.

He says, "This whole thing doesn't feel right."

"What thing?" Tom says.

"This arrangement. Now Marilyn is dead, you living under my roof; she must be turning in her grave."

"She's dead, Walter, she doesn't care what we do."

Something explodes inside Walter. "You can be so heartless sometimes." The bitterness and anger he has kept inside for the past half hour is now coming to the surface. He stands from the bench and walks away. He can't deal with Tom and his know-everything attitude.

"Fuck!" Tom says under his breath.

He catches up to Walter who stops in front of an ice cream kiosk.

Walter gets a pistachio and chocolate ice cream from the vendor. He turns to Tom and says, "Do you want an ice cream?" He tries to remain calm and in control of his anger.

Tom moves closer to him. "I'm sorry, I just don't want you to think it's our fault Marilyn killed herself."

Walter takes his change from the vendor. He takes a lick from his ice cream and walks away.

Tom follows him and catches up with him.

"It would be to simple to think the only reason why she killed herself was because of our relationship," Tom says.

Walter stops and turns to Tom. "What do you know, anyway? You're barely twenty, you don't know what love is. You don't know what it's like to burn for someone."

Tom seems a little stunned. "You think I've never been in love with anyone?"

"It was not love, just your hormones."

Tom stands in front of Walter and stops him from walking. "What does age have to do with love? Are you telling me just because I am young, I don't have any feelings?"

"No, Tom, I'm saying until you've been burnt, you don't have any appreciation of love, you think it's just a game."

Tom is struggling a little for a reply. "You want me to move out?"

"Not what I said."

"No, but you're getting there."

"You can be so childish sometimes."

"Childish?"

Tom moves forward and knocks Walter's ice cream to the ground. "Childish enough for you?"

Walter is totally floored. It's obvious he didn't expect this. There is so much going on in his mind right now, he can't deal with any more disagreements. "I—"

"Fuck you! You want me to go, I'll go."

Tom storms off.

Walter is left standing embarrassed with his ice cream on the ground.

Why do I keep doing this to myself?

A pug comes along and eats the ice cream from the ground. Walter looks at it and thinks how easy a dog's life must be compared to his.

He watches Tom vanish in the distance, past the bench they sat on a moment ago, past the high steel gate and into the botanical gardens.

CHAPTER TEN

Walter is facing the camera.

"I know it was wrong to take my anger out on Tom," he says. "After all, I'm the one who told him he could stay at my place for as long as he wants."

"Has he moved out yet?" the interviewer asks.

"The same night."

"Do you know where to?"

"Didn't say. When I got home, he had cleared everything out of the room. Didn't even leave a note."

"How does it make you feel?"

"Like I've betrayed him, like I've betrayed myself. Maybe I'm the one who's childish." He puts his head down and then looks up again. "I've never been good with understanding people. I don't even think I understand myself at times. I'm such a mess of emotions and confusion."

"Have you thought about getting some professional help?"

"In what way?"

"Counselling."

"I don't need counselling."

"Marilyn has killed herself, and you've just told me you're a mess of emotions and confusion."

Walter thinks for a few seconds. "I'm not comfortable talking about my private life."

"You seem to be doing fine right at this moment."

"It's not the same, it's just a camera, not a shrink. If they find there is something wrong with me, they're going to medicate me—I don't want to be medicated. You know what modern medicine does to people? Didn't you hear what Tom Cruise said?"

"I'm sorry?"

"The show where Tom Cruise was saying psychiatry and medication are harmful."

"Oh, yes, I think I might have seen it on YouTube."

"Well, everyone thinks Tom Cruise is a nut-case when he made the comment, but I think he was spot on."

"That psychiatry is dangerous?"

"And medicating people."

"Okay."

There is an awkward silence for a few seconds.

"And how is Lucia coping with all this?" the interviewer finally says. "She was Marilyn's best friend after all."

"I don't really know Lucia all well. Like you've said, she was Marilyn's friend." He thinks the question over. "I think she's back with Nathan. She begged him apparently, and he was willing to give the relationship another go. It's what love does to people; it blinds them totally. She always struck me as real cunning, but like I've said, I don't really know her."

CHAPTER ELEVEN

Nathan is lying in bed. The white sheet is covering the bottom half of his body. He has just woken up from a deep sleep. The night before he had sex with Lucia again and after he slept like a baby. Sex always drains him out of energy. He read somewhere it's the reason why men have a shorter life expectancy than women—because they lose energy every time they have sex when they release their seeds and pass them on to their lovers. Women take the energy. Men lose it forever.

From the corner of his eye, he can see Lucia stepping out of the shower. She always leaves the door half open because the fan in the bathroom is not adequate enough to suck the hot steam out of the room. He has the same problem when he has a shower, and when he has to shave, he can't even see himself clearly in the mirror.

Lucia dries herself with a pink towel. Her body is still very toned up for someone who is over forty. Her breasts are not even sagging and her legs are thin and muscular at the calves. When she turns around slightly, he sees her dark pubic hair, and suddenly he grows an erection, forcing the sheet covering him to move vertically away from his body.

He says, "Did you leave enough hot water for me?"

"Yes," Lucia replies.

She walks up to the vanity mirror, sits on a chair, drops her towel and fixes her make-up and hair. She is totally naked from the back, and he can see the fullness of her arse. His erection is growing even stronger now, the lower part of the sheet looking like a tent.

He massages his dick and says, "Are you going to be late tonight?"

"Maybe. I'm not sure."

Silence for a few seconds.

Then Lucia says, "I'm not seeing Lorenzo if it's what you're getting at."

"I was just wondering if I should have something ready for dinner?"

Lucia looks over her shoulder and smiles at him. "Why don't I call you later in the day and let you know how I'm progressing?"

Nathan stands from the bed and walks to where Lucia is sitting, his erection hard like a rock. He massages her back with his hands.

Lucia says, "I'm kind of busy right now, I have to get ready for work."

He slides his hands from behind her back, past her rib cage, and stops at her chest. He cups her breasts with both hands and pushes his erection between her bum cheeks.

Lucia seems a little annoyed.

"Maybe you can start work a little later today?" Nathan says.

"Not today."

Nathan kisses her on the nap of the neck. "It's going to be a long day without you. Give me a taste of something to look forward to."

Lucia looks at his reflection in the mirror. "This is the third time this week I'm going to be late. I'm going to lose my job because of you."

"And so what if you lose your job? We'll be poor, but at least we'll be together and happy."

He forces her head around with his right hand and kisses

her on the cheek and gently drifts to her mouth.

They kiss passionately and then pull back.

She looks down and notices his erection.

"You've got five minutes, not a second more," she says.

He pulls her into the bed and pushes her back against the mattress. He can't wait any longer and skips the foreplay. With both hands, he pulls her knees apart and stares for a few seconds at the darkness of her bush.

When he enters her, he knows she's not ready yet, but he doesn't care. He jack-hammers away and releases all the love from inside him into her, and when he's done, he rests his face on her chest, his mouth only half an inch away from her right nipple. Being close to her is so wonderful, but at the same time he doesn't like the fact he has to depend so much on her for his own well-being.

As he stares at the fold of her right breast, he finally realises he loves women as much as he hates them.

CHAPTER TWELVE

Nathan is facing the camera. He looks happier than he was in the earlier interviews. He is also well shaved, and he doesn't smoke.

He says, "After I agreed she could move in with me again, she really made an effort. We made love every night for the first week."

"And how did it make you feel?" the interviewer asks.

"Good. Real good. I hadn't felt like this since we began dating back at University."

"What about her? How does she feel?

"Happy, I guess. She's always smiling."

"So you're in love all over again?"

"She's the love of my life. She's always been the love of my life."

"But you kicked her out of home only a couple of weeks ago."

"You can't share someone you love with someone else."

"Why not? Sometimes people have lovers, and they stay true to their relationship."

"How can you be true to a relationship if you have a lover?"

"The French do it."

"I'm not French."

"I know you're not French."

"I'm sorry, but you've lost me. What exactly is the point you're trying to make?"

"I'm not making a point. I'm just trying to make you think about what you've just said."

"About lovers?"

"Yes."

"Okay, well, I'm not French, and I don't think a couple in a relationship can last if one of them has a lover on the side."

"Is this from your personal experience?"

"Well, yes and no. It didn't work out with Lucia when she was sleeping with Lorenzo, and look at what's happened to Marilyn? Why do you think she's killed herself? Because she couldn't get back with Walter. You know why she left Walter in the first place?"

"Maybe I do, but I can't really get into details with you."

"Okay, it's confidential, I know. Well, she left him because he was having an affair with a man. How do you think it made her feel?" Nathan shakes his head. "Like she wasn't good enough, like he didn't find her attractive enough, like she was just some piece of furniture in the house."

"You're feeling very passionate about this?"

"It's not a matter of passion. It's a matter of having gone through hell and back. If you've ever been betrayed by someone you love, then you'll know what I'm talking about."

CHAPTER THIRTEEN

Nathan and Samantha are having coffee at the local coffee shop. It's early afternoon, and there are another two customers at tables nearby having coffee and coke. Outside it's overcast, and it smells like rain in the distance, even though the temperature is mild.

Samantha says, "Everyone has been hurt by love." She wears jeans and a white top and a little too much make-up.

"What about you?" Nathan says.

Samantha smiles. "Yes, me too."

A few seconds of silence.

Nathan says, "Is this why I've never seen you with anyone?"

"Maybe."

"You don't give much away, do you?"

"I like to keep to myself."

Nathan sips from his coffee. "Maybe it's the best thing to do."

Samantha shifts on her chair. "So, how are you going with Lucia?"

"Good. I'm making dinner for the both of us tonight."

"What about the affair you think she was having?"

"I think it's over, I *hope* it's over."

Samantha places her right hand on top of Nathan's left hand. "Well, I'm glad to hear you're back together."

"Me too."

CHAPTER FOURTEEN

Nathan is seated at the kitchen table. There are two plates with food untouched—orange glazed chicken, baked potatoes and zucchini. He looks clearly upset. He has already drunk half the bottle of red wine. The dinner he has prepared is now beyond saving. He could have worked on his novel for two hours, but instead he used his creative time cooking for the both of them. He had been looking forward to their dinner together and hoped it would be the beginning of a new phase in their relationship.

The sex they had this morning has been on his mind all day, and he jerked off twice over the bathroom hand-sink just thinking about her. Actually, he was more thinking about her vagina and tits than her, and it's what really drove him into a state of sexual frenzy when he relieved himself all over the sink.

He hears the front door of the apartment and checks his watch.

Where the fuck has she been?

"Nathan?" Lucia yells out.

He is too upset to reply.

Lucia appears in the kitchen. She's dressed with her work clothes—black skirt and matching jacket and a white blouse—and carries a leather-bound briefcase by her side. He notices she's not wearing her shoes.

She says, "I'm sorry I'm late. I got held back."

"You told me you'd be here two hours ago?"

Lucia looks at her watch. "I didn't realise it was so late."

She sees the food on the table. "I'm so sorry. I should have called you back, but it was impossible, I was with a client, and there was no way I could get to a phone."

"You could have texted me."

"I left the phone on my desk. Sorry."

She puts her briefcase on the floor and removes her jacket. She hangs the jacket at the back of a kitchen chair.

She sits at the table. "Thanks for cooking."

Nathan says, "It's going to taste like shit. It's been ready for a couple of hours."

Lucia takes a bite from her plate. "It tastes fine. Really, it tastes great."

She chews slowly, and it's obvious she doesn't mean what she's just said.

Nathan glares at her. Right now, he could just grab the fork to the right of his plate and stick it in her eye. Her cocky smile really annoys her at times, this self-righteous shit she does all the time, an excuse for every action, as if she were the only person who mattered.

She says, "Okay, it's a bit cold, but just a few seconds in the microwave..."

She grabs her plate and then Nathan's.

When she gets Nathan's plate halfway up from the table, he pushes it and says, "It's gonna taste like shit, even if you microwave it!"

The plate falls to the floor and shatters in pieces, the sound like a gunshot.

Lucia stands with only one plate in her hands, somewhat shocked at what has happened and the anger coming out of Nathan.

Nathan doesn't move.

Lucia says, "You...mmm...I..."

"Fuck this!" Nathan screams. "You told me you'd be here two hours ago! I've spent my afternoon cooking because you told me you would be home on time. You lied to me!"

"I didn't lie. Things got busy at work."

She places her plate carefully back on the table, away from Nathan.

"Busy, euh? Is this starting all over? Are you seeing Lorenzo again?"

"I'm not seeing Lorenzo. That part of my life is truly over."

An awkward silence.

Lucia says, "I can get pizza if you want?"

Nathan sulks.

"Tony Pepperoni, your favourite."

Nathan looks at her.

"And then we'll fuck like rabbits?" she says and smiles.

He keeps staring at her.

Sexual bait.

Here we go again.

And it's why they say men think with their dicks, and women know it.

"Please...?" Lucia said, and he pretends in his mind she's saying *please, can you fuck me?*

He smiles back. "You're driving me crazy, you know?"

She comes close to him and ruffles his hair. "Oh, baby is grumpy."

He wraps his arms around her waist. Damn it, he's been waiting all day for this. He is going to fuck her right here on the kitchen table. Come to think of it, they've never done it on the kitchen table. It will be just like in the movie *9½ Weeks* with Mickey Rourke and Kim Basinger, food all over the table, condiments used as sex toys. He's getting hard just thinking about it.

Just as Lucia moves forward to get closer to him, she jumps on the spot. "Ouch!" She looks down. "Fuck!"

There's blood on the floor, coming from underneath her

stocking.

She says, "I cut myself on the broken plate."

"Let me look at it," Nathan says calmly.

They move to the bathroom virtually attached to the kitchen.

Lucia is sits on the edge of the bathtub.

Nathan washes the cut under her foot in cold water with a hand-held shower head. There's blood running with the water into the bathtub's drain.

Lucia grimaces. "Ouch!"

Nathan turns the tap off. "Let's have a closer look." He lifts her foot and looks. "There's still a piece stuck in there. Hold on a sec——"

He turns to the hand sink, opens the mirrored cabinet above and removes a pair of silver tweezers.

He sits back on the edge of the bathtub, just next to Lucia. "Let me have a look."

He takes her foot and lines up the wound with his eyesight.

Lucia says, "Maybe we should go to the hospital."

"It's nothing," Nathan says, "I can see it. I can get it out."

He digs into the wound and clamps the shattered piece of plate with the tweezers.

"Fuck! It hurts." Lucia says.

Nathan is very focused on what he's doing. "I got it, I got it!" He pulls out the piece from her foot. "Done!"

"Jesus Christ! It hurts like hell!"

Nathan looks with fascination at the broken piece of plate. "Look at the size of it!"

Lucia tries to stand, but she can't put her foot on the floor flat. "How am I supposed to be at work tomorrow? I can't even stand up!"

Nathan lifts the piece of broken plate to the ceiling light so he can examine it better. "I can't believe you had this in your foot. It's huge."

Lucia hops to the door frame. "Fuck, Nathan, you and your

temper. I'm going to look like an idiot."

"Amazing," Nathan says.

CHAPTER FIFTEEN

Lorenzo is making himself a cup of coffee. It's just on 10 a.m. at the office where he works, and there's a big day ahead of him. If it weren't for work, he'll go crazy thinking too much about Lucia, Tom and all the people in his life who are becoming too much for him to handle.

Lucia walks in with crutches. She has a bandage on her right foot. She seems really irritated, and Lorenzo can feel the electrical tension in the air, even though she hasn't said a word yet.

He says, "What the hell happened to you?"

She struggles to get to the table.

Lorenzo stops what he's doing. "Hold on, let me help you."

He pulls back a chair and helps her to sit down.

She sits down. She tosses the crutches on the floor and rubs her armpits and says, "Shit, those things hurt like hell!"

Lorenzo sits at the table next to her. "What happened?"

"Nathan had one of his fits again."

"Did he hit you?"

"No, he broke a plate, and I stepped on it."

Lorenzo looks at the bandaged foot. "Does it hurt?"

"Yeah, it bloody hurts, what do you think?"

Lorenzo puts his hands up. "Hey, don't get shitty with me. I'm not the one who broke the plate."

Lucia places her hands on the tabletop. "I'm sorry, I've had

71

a really bad night, and I have to meet with Gordon today, and look at the state I'm in. How am I supposed to make an impression? This is just ridiculous. Look at my jacket. It looks as if a cow has chewed on it!"

"I can meet with Gordon if you want."

She looks at him for a few seconds and considers the proposition he's just made. Finally, she purses her lips and says, "You're too young."

"Too young for what?"

"I've worked hard to get this contract, and, no offence, I don't want you to fuck it up."

"Thanks for the vote of confidence."

She think it over for a few seconds. "Do you think you can handle it?"

"Well, yeah, otherwise I wouldn't be asking," he says.

She stares at him. "Okay, but if you fuck this up, I'm going to kill both you and Nathan."

Lorenzo stands from his chair. "I'm the good guy here."

"There's no such thing as a good guy."

Lorenzo shakes his head and moves to the bench to finish his coffee making.

Fuckin women!

She says, "And make me a coffee while you are there, and make it strong. I feel like shit, and I'm going to need as much caffeine as my heart can tolerate."

Lorenzo obeys and makes two coffees.

Six hours later, they are at his apartment, her on the bed, one leg up, her panties down and him entering her full frontal.

He wants so badly to be left alone and be in control of his own sexual life, but he's too weak even though he thinks if he tries hard enough, he can walk away from all this.

When he enters her, she closes her eyes and hold on tight to his back. She seems totally lost in his lovemaking, and it's why it's making it so hard to walk away from everything, but at the same time, he feels used and *dirty*.

When he finally comes, a part of his soul is gone with him, and he knows this will have to end eventually, but he just doesn't have what it takes to leave her.

CHAPTER SIXTEEN

Lucia is facing the camera.

"Lorenzo and I stopped fucking the day I moved back with Nathan. I know Lorenzo has a hard time accepting what was happening, but at least we remain friends." She lies but she doesn't care. She's over this university research project.

"Do you miss making love to Lorenzo?" the interviewer asks.

She brings her hand up to her face to move a strand of hair and can smell his sex on her fingertips.

"Not at all," she says.

"You're not lying to me, are you? It's really important you tell the truth, or the whole research will become pointless."

"I'm not lying."

"So you've never made love to him again?"

"Okay, once...maybe."

"You want to tell me about it."

"Not really."

"But it would help us tremendously with the research. After all it's what we're paying you for."

She thinks for a few seconds. "You know I don't really need the money, with my job and everything. I only agreed to do this because Nathan, Marilyn and Walter talked me into it."

"I understand, but you've signed a contract, and I think it's kind of important we stick to the contract. We've only got one week to go."

Lucia takes a sip of water from a bottle on the table. "Okay, fuck it, what is it you want to know?"

"I want to know if you continued to have a relationship with Lorenzo behind Nathan's back after you moved back with Nathan."

"I wouldn't call it a relationship."

"What would you call it then?"

"We fucked."

"Once, twice, three times?"

"Once. It was the first day I went to work on crutches. He sealed the deal with Gordon, and I was very proud of him."

"And?"

"And I fucked him because I was proud of him, my way of saying thank you."

"I see..."

There's an awkward silence.

Lucia says, "What the fuck is this supposed to mean? I'm not a whore. I fucked him because I wanted to fuck him"

"I didn't say you were a whore."

"No, but you're implying it. I fucked Lorenzo because he is in love with me, and it means something to me, okay?"

"Okay, fine." He looks down at this notes and then up again. "And did you tell Nathan?"

"About what?"

"You making love to Lorenzo?"

"What are you? Out of your fuckin' mind?"

"I'm sorry, but I think it's better if we finish for today; you're becoming increasingly aggres-sive."

"Fine with me. I hate doing this shit, anyway."

She stands from the chair and leaves the room.

CHAPTER SEVENTEEN

Lucia and Samantha are having coffee at their usual coffee place. It's late afternoon, and Lucia left work early to see a doctor because the cut in her foot is not healing properly. The doctor told her there was some infection, so he gave her some antibiotics.

Lucia takes a sip from her coffee and says, "I never told you about the research?

"No," Samantha says.

"It's some university research about people in relationships. I'm not supposed to talk about it."

"So why are you telling me?"

"Because the person who is conducting the interview is getting really intrusive. He's pushing my buttons."

Samantha locks eyes with her. "Don't go back there."

"It's only for one more week."

"Okay."

"But you know what I don't get?"

Samantha shrugs.

"I don't understand why he's filming me and telling me no one will see the recording except him."

"Maybe it's true."

"Why doesn't he just take notes then?"

"Did you sign a contract of some sort?"

"Yes, but it was all fine print, and you know, like an idiot I signed it. And I'm a lawyer, I should have known better."

"If you have any concerns, you should check with the faculty funding the research."

Lucia thinks this over for a few seconds. "You know, it's a really good idea." She looks down to the table top and then back up at Samantha. "I told this bastard I was pregnant."

"Oh, my God, congratulations."

"Yes, but, I told him I thought it was Lorenzo's baby, not Nathan's."

"Well..."

"So now I'm scared if he uploads those interviews on the Internet, Nathan is going to find out I'm pregnant with Lorenzo's baby."

"Wow! You really need to do something about this."

Lucia stares at an invisible spot. "I think you're right. I need to put an end to this."

They talk some more about her foot injury, and how it's going to take a couple of months to heal properly. She should have gone to emergency in the first place instead of listening to Nathan on how it wasn't such a big deal. She hates him so much at times, but she also knows she's not getting any younger, and now would not be a good time to end a relationship. Women over forty have a very hard time trying to find a man who is going to settle with them for the rest of their lives.

Hang on to what you've got.

When they leave the cafe, rain comes pouring down like a torrent.

CHAPTER EIGHTEEN

Tom and Lorenzo are having a beer at the bar of a local nightclub. Techno is playing in the background and young people are shaking it on the dance floor. It's early in the night, and the crowd is quite thin, but early birds don't pay the entrance fee and take advantage of the situation.

Tom says, "I don't understand where you're going with all this. One minute you're telling me it's over with Lucia, the next you're back with her again."

"I don't expect you to understand," Lorenzo says. "It's complicated."

"It's not."

"You don't know what it's like when someone's attached to you."

"What about Walter? He doesn't count?"

Lorenzo takes a slow sip from his beer. "I'm worried about her."

"What about?"

"How she's making the wrong choice by going back to Nathan."

"Well, it would depend on what she gets out of the relationship."

"She's sleeping with him again."

Tom shakes his head and takes a sip from his beer. "Oh, man, this is getting really messy. Does he know she's still seeing you?"

"Don't think so, but if he finds out."

Tom stands from his chair. "You should break it off and forget about the whole thing."

"I'm in love with her."

"You've already told me. Just because you're in love with someone, it doesn't mean you should be with her."

"What are you talking about?"

"People fall in love with the wrong person every day. And if they persist on being with the wrong person, they end up fucking up their lives."

Tom finishes his beer.

Lorenzo is about to reply, but Tom cuts in first. "Look, I got to go. I need a place to stay, and I can't go back to my parents, and I can't go back to Walter."

"I wish I could help, but you know..."

"Thanks, anyway. I'll manage."

Tom leaves the bar.

Lorenzo is sitting by himself with his beer.

Maybe Tom is right. This is just to messy to continue with. It might be best to just leave everything and start all over again somewhere else, a place where nobody knows him, and where he won't find himself hurting others.

CHAPTER NINETEEN

Lorenzo is facing the camera. He is smoking. He's just picked up the habit, and it's the first time he's been smoking in years. He began at high school through peer pressure but stopped the same year because he couldn't afford the cost of the cigarettes.

He says, "I'm completely at a loss as to what to do."

"I guess it all depends if you feel it's wrong you're sleeping with someone who's in a relationship with another person," the interviewer says.

"But you see, she wasn't really in a relationship anymore. She'd left him, and now she's back with him, but somehow she won't let go of me."

"And you think it's a problem?"

"Well, hell, yes, it's a problem. I don't want to be in the middle of this mess. It's all going to end up badly one day. Look what happened to Marilyn. You always see it in films. Someone ends up dying in the end."

"But films are not reality."

"True, but what's reality?"

"What is reality? What do you think?"

"I guess it's what you make it. It's a perception thing, isn't it."

The interviewer writers something in his pad. "What does Lucia think of all this?"

"Honestly? I'm not sure anymore." He takes a drag from

80

his cigarette. "You don't mind if I smoke, do you?"

"No, it's fine."

"You know what I think I'm gonna do?"

"What are you going to do?"

"I'm going to leave this town—I'm just going to pack everything and start somewhere all over again."

"And you think it would solve all the problems?"

"If I'm not here, Lucia won't be having an affair with anyone. She'll be faithful to Nathan. She can marry him without wondering if she's just being a bitch. And I won't feel rotten about the whole thing."

"So you feel bad about sleeping with Lucia behind Nathan's back?"

"Yeah, I guess I do. I'm tired of being the third wheel."

"What about Tom?"

"Maybe he can come with me?"

"Did you talk to him?"

"No, but he's got nowhere to go. He's homeless, so starting afresh somewhere new is better than fading away."

"Are you in love with Tom?"

Lorenzo ponders the question for a few seconds and then says, "With Tom, there's only one big problem."

"What's?"

"I don't want to be gay."

"I'm sorry, but didn't you say the other day you are bi-sexual?"

"Correct, and because I have a choice, I'd rather not be gay."

"Why?"

"Because gay people have an incredibly hard time being accepted in society. It's easier to fit in when people don't perceive you as gay. I can just pretend to be straight. Most people think I am anyway. Lucia doesn't even know I'm seeing Tom."

"Do you think Tom is going to be okay? You know, with

finding a place to stay?"

"He's got plenty of friends. I'm sure he's having a nice hot shower as we speak."

"Okay, well, try not to leave town before the end of the month. We're nearly done here."

CHAPTER TWENTY

It's early morning and freezing cold. Tom has been sleeping on a bench in the park near the Williamstown Botanical Gardens for the entire night. He's never done this before, and he'd hardly slept. The bench is steel hard, and he can feel the discomfort from sleeping all night on it through every bone in his body. He's sure he's going to catch a cold. Even though it hasn't been raining, dampness has seeped through his skin and into his bones.

Painfully, he sits up on the bench and looks around. It's deserted, other than a man walking his dog in the distance. He can't make out the breed of the dog, but it looks mid-size, maybe a border collie or similar.

He wraps his arms around his body and wishes he had hot coffee with him right now. How easy it is to be ungrateful for the simpler things in life—a bedroom, a pillow, a shower, a good coffee, a conversation, the soft touch of another human being.

Tom stands from the bench and walks down the park. Morning light is creeping in, and already it's not as dark as when he woke up ten minutes ago.

He sees someone walking towards him. The shape of the man is familiar, and he senses his adrenalin kicking in like a six sense of knowing.

When the walker gets closer, he notices it's Walter. Shit, it's the last person in the world he wants to see.

Walter notices him to and yells out, "Hey, Tom! What are you doing here?"

Tom stands where he is and looks right and left as if there is a possibility to hide somewhere without Walter seeing him.

Walter walks up to him. "Oh, my God, you look like shit."

Tom just stares at Walter. Tom looks like he's about cry. He is trembling from the cold and the lack of sleep.

Walter says, "Jesus, you're freezing." Walter removes his jacket and wraps it around Tom. "Did you sleep here last night?"

Tom says, "Couldn't find a place."

"You should have come to me."

Tom walks with his head down. "I need to get out of here —"

"Come and stay with me until you find your own place."

"I don't think so. It's never going to work out. I'm always going to be the reason why Marilyn killed herself."

Walter puts his arms around Tom.

Tom pushes him back. "Just leave me alone, okay?" There is anger in his voice. He pushes Walter back with the palm of both hands.

"Tom, I—"

"Go away. I don't want to be with you. I don't want all this, I don't want to depend on someone else for my happiness."

"You're just stressed. Come home and sleep it off."

Tom removes the jacket Walter has given him and throws it back at him. "Go away. Leave me alone."

Walter is floored. "Don't do this. You know how I feel about you."

"I don't feel the same about you, so just go."

Walter looks as if he's about to cry. He picks up his coat from the ground.

Tom turns around and walks in the other direction.

Walter is left by himself in the park like a lost dog with nowhere to go.

CHAPTER TWENTY-ONE

Tom is facing the camera. He hasn't shaved for a few days. His hair is a mess. He's drinking hot coffee.

The interviewer says, "And you think cutting Walter out of your life completely will solve anything?"

"I don't know. All I know is I need to move on. And this town is suffocating me. I can't breathe." He empties his cup of coffee.

"You want a refill?" the interviewer asks, the coffee pot already in his hand.

Tom says, "Sure. It's cold in here."

The interviewer refills the cup. "The heater's broken down."

"Thanks."

"You're welcome."

Tom holds the warm mug with both hands and takes in a mouthful of coffee.

"Did Lorenzo talk to you?" the interviewer says.

"About what?"

"Leaving town. He's saying what you're saying. He needs to get out of this town."

"Yeah, we talked about it, it's an option I guess."

"Did he say anything to you about not wanting to be gay?"

"What do you mean?"

"He didn't say anything?"

"Hey, didn't you say what we told you in this room was confidential?"

"I'm sorry, I thought he might have mentioned it, otherwise I wouldn't have said anything."

"Well, what did he say?"

"He'd rather not be gay."

"Fuck, bloody hell, find the easy way out."

"Does it bother you?"

Tom thinks this over for a few seconds. "Why would it bother me? It's not like I've got a choice."

"It's what I mean."

"I'm not in love with him. We're just really good friends. So he can do what he wants. It's not going to spoil our friendship."

"Okay, so if he asks you to leave town with him, would you do it?"

"Yeah, if he asked me, I would."

CHAPTER TWENTY-TWO

Tom is helping Lorenzo to pack his personal belongings in bags and suitcases. They are in Lorenzo's room and decided the night before to leave town together and start somewhere else, away from their lovers and families. They concluded you cannot grow as a man unless you become totally independent.

Tom holds up a red, leather body-building belt. "Where do you want me to put this?"

Lorenzo looks at it for a few seconds. "Just leave it here. It's going to take too much room in the suitcase."

"Can I have it?"

Lorenzo hesitates. "Sure. But you're not taking it with you, are you?"

"Of course, it's why I want it."

"In this case, I'll keep it"

Lorenzo grabs the belt from Tom.

Tom says, "Jeez, thanks a lot."

Fifteen minutes later they are standing at a bus stop, suitcases and bags at their feet. They are both wearing jeans and hoodies. The sky is a perfect blue and the air warm and smells of freshly cut grass.

Tom says, "Do your parents know you're leaving?"

"I left them a note," Lorenzo says.

"Just a note?"

"I'll ring them when we get to wherever we're going."

"I don't want to come back here—ever."

The bus appears over the hill and comes crawling to a stop right in front of where they are sitting.

"Well, this is," Tom says.

Lorenzo smiles. "Goodbye, cruel world."

He goes in first and Tom follows.

Tom says, "Do you think we're doing the right thing?"

"Yes, fuck them all."

Tom smiles and climbs the last steps of the bus.

CHAPTER TWENTY-THREE

Lucia and Walter are having coffee at Lucia's favorite coffee place.

"What's he going to do with the recordings?" Lucia says.

Walter looks at her straight on. "Didn't tell me, kept on saying it's for research, but he's been very vague about everything else."

Lucia takes a sip from her coffee. "I don't understand, if it's for research, then why does he keep on saying no one other than himself will be watching the recordings?"

"You now what I think?"

"What?"

"I think we should ask him for the recordings. You never know where they're going to end up."

"What do you mean?"

"Haven't you heard of YouTube?"

"Who hasn't?"

"How do we know he's not going to upload the recordings on YouTube? And then what? Do you really want Nathan to know what you've been saying?"

Lucia finishes the rest of her coffee. "You don't think he's just going to hand them over because we're asking?"

"I don't suppose he will, no."

They take a break in the conversation for thirty seconds.

Lucia says, "Things are going well with Nathan at the

moment—I can't afford to have those videos made public."

"What are we going to do?" Walter asks.

"Leave it to me. I'll work it out."

"What are you going to do?"

"Put an end to it."

CHAPTER TWENTY-FOUR

In the lounge room of their high-rise apartment, Lucia is sitting on a chair, her injured foot up another chair. Nathan is examining the foot.

"It's healing well," he says. "Can you walk without the crutches?"

"I've tried, but it hurts like hell. I'm scared if I put too much pressure on it, the wound will open up."

Nathan takes a cotton pad from the kitchen table, puts some antiseptic on it and wipes Lucia's wound. "What if I double the bandage? It would give you more padding."

Lucia stares at him for a few seconds, looking as if she's going to lose it, but then she smiles. "Sure, it might work."

Nathan takes some bandage from the kitchen table and dresses her foot.

Lucia says, "I've been thinking about every-thing we've gone through, and firstly I want to say I'm sorry with what happened with Lorenzo."

Nathan focuses on his task. "I thought we were not going to talk about him anymore."

"Just hear me out."

Nathan looks up. "Okay. What?"

"Lorenzo is leaving town permanently."

"And?"

"And I'll never see him again."

An awkward silence.

Nathan says, "You're telling me if he was staying in town, you might go back to him?"

Nathan's question stops her dead.

They stare at each other for a few seconds.

Finally, Lucia says, "I just think it's time for us to make a more serious commitment to our relationship."

Nathan tightens the bandage on her foot really hard. If it had been around her neck, he would have strangled her.

"It hurts," Lucia says, aggravation in her tone. "Can you loosen it a bit?"

"Sorry." He undoes the bandage and tries again. "You were saying? About commitment?"

"I want us to get married."

Nathan stops what he's doing. He looks up at her. "Are you serious?"

She smiles. "Yes."

"This is not another one of your tricks?"

"I'm asking you to marry me, Nathan. I want to spend the rest of my life with you."

Nathan is stunned.

"I'm pregnant," she says.

They stare at one another for a few seconds.

Nathan says, "Wow, wonderful. So it's really over with Lorenzo?"

"I'm having your baby. It's why I want to get married. I made my choice."

Nathan moves close to her. "Yes."

"Yes, what?"

"Yes, I'll marry you."

They kiss.

Thirty minutes later they are in bed.

"I got to take a pee," Nathan says and gets up from the bed. He is naked, but it doesn't seem to worry him. He goes to the bathroom.

Lucia steps of the bed and goes to the built-in wardrobe. She opens the door and retrieves the handgun Marilyn killed herself with.

Lucia crosses the bedroom and puts the gun in her handbag. She goes back to bed.

Nathan walks back into the room.

"Everything okay?" he asks.

"Yes, why?"

"I don't know, you've got this look on your face."

"I'm just tired."

He joins Lucia in bed.

Nathan moves on to Lucia and forces her into another lovemaking session.

CHAPTER TWENTY-FIVE

Nathan is facing the camera. He is clean shaven and neatly dressed. He looks refreshed and happy.

"She said she would never see him again," he says.

"And you believe her?" the interviewer says.

"I want to believe her, I need to believe her."

"And you think getting married is going to solve the fact she's been unfaithful to you?"

"Yes. We were not married before. She never said she would be faithful to me, but marriage, it's different. You make a promise of faithfulness in front of witnesses."

"What if she cheats on you again?"

"She won't."

"You don't know for sure."

"Neither do you."

"Fair enough....I just want to let you know people don't really change. They might for a short time, but then they go back to being themselves."

"I'm sorry, but I thought this research of yours was supposed to be interview-based? You're preaching to me."

"You're right. I'm out of line. I'm just concerned you're placing too much faith in Lucia."

"I'm leaving now. This is my last session, isn't it?"

"Yes, you've fulfilled your contractual obligation. You may leave if you wish."

"Honestly, I don't know what the point of all this was."

"It's just research."

"For what?"

"Relationship research. You know, how people react to one another and do the things they do."

"I'm wondering how much of this is your fault."

"My fault? What do you mean?" The interviewer seems genuinely shocked.

"Marilyn killed herself, and she was one of your research subjects."

"I didn't make her kill herself. She killed herself because of her husband."

"But surely, you must have seen she was distressed, you must have known she was suicidal since you've been speaking to her for weeks."

"I give you my word she never said anything about committing suicide. In fact, when I last saw her, she was really happy and looked as if her life was back on track."

"Somebody died because of you, It's what I think."

"I'm sorry you feel this way."

CHAPTER TWENTY-SIX

Walter visits Marilyn's grave at the St Kilda cemetery. It's a cloudy day, and the cold cuts through his black coat. There is not a single soul in sight.

He kneels down in the grass patch in front of the stone grave, unable to understand where he is and how Marilyn is in there, in the dirt, never to be seen again.

He begins to sob uncontrollably and lets hot tears roll down his eyes. He has never felt so miserable in his life because it's the first time he loses someone who has been so closer to him for so long. The tearing in his heart rips his soul in half.

How did it come to this?

There is so much he could have done, but now it's too late. He's never going to recover from this, and he knows it. It's going to be his life story, what he is going to be remembered for. The bastard who cheated on his wife with a man, deprived her of the love they used to share, and let her kill herself when he took it all back from her.

What a total fuckin' useless arsehole of a man am I?

CHAPTER TWENTY-SEVEN

Nathan, Lucia, Samantha and Walter are having dinner at Walter's place. They are all seated around an oak dinner table, dressed for the occasion. The dish for the evening is lamb roast, peas, carrots and baked potatoes with a garden salad.

Lucia says, "I'm telling you, there's something not right about this research."

"I agree with her," Walter says.

Eyes cross the table.

Nathan says, "Aren't you being a little paranoid?"

"You just said you've told him it's probably his fault Marilyn killed herself," Lucia says.

"Yes, but it's because I was angry. It doesn't mean he killed her on purpose. Maybe we're all over-reacting."

Walter looks upset.

"I'm sorry," Lucia says to Walter.

"It's all right," Walter says.

"So you're basically concerned how the recordings of the interviews are going to end up on the Internet or somewhere public?" Samantha says.

"Yes," Lucia says.

"He said it was confidential," Nathan says.

"Oh, right, haven't I heard this one before," Lucia says.

They stay silent for a few seconds.

Walter says, "Lucia is right. I think we should get the

recordings."

"He's not going to just hand them over," Samantha says.

"I still think you're overreacting," Nathan says.

"I've got to see him tomorrow, anyway," Lucia says. "I am going to get to the bottom of this one way or another."

CHAPTER TWENTY-EIGHT

Lucia is facing the camera. Her hair is a mess, and she looks really angry. There's a handbag on the table.

She says, "Who else is going to view these recordings?"

"No one. Just me. It's private research," the interviewer says.

Lucia looks somewhere to the right and sees a pile of digital versatile discs. "Are those the recordings?"

"Yes."

"All of them?"

"Yes. "

"Give them to me."

"I don't think I can."

She reaches into her bag and pulls a gun, the same gun she gave Marilyn, the one Marilyn killed herself with. She aims the gun at the camera.

"Turn the fucking camera off and give me the discs," she orders.

The interviewer reaches for the digital versatile discs and tosses them over the tabletop to where Lucia is sitting.

Lucia says, "And turn the fucking camera off, I said."

"Okay, okay, just put the gun down." There is genuine fear in his eyes.

"Do you get some kind of enjoyment from peeping into people's lives? Do you have idea how much pain you've caused?"

"I told you it was research—"

"Research, my arse. I've checked with the Faculty of Human Behaviour, they've never heard about your research."

"It's not classified."

"What the fuck are you talking about?"

"It's a secret research, it hasn't got depart-mental approval."

"So, no one knows about this?"

"No."

"Not a single person?"

"Well, other than you and the other people I interviewed."

"No one else?"

"No."

"Is the fucking camera off yet?"

The interviewer reaches over and switches off the camera. The recording red light is no longer on.

"It's switched off," he says.

"Are you sure?"

"Yes."

"Good."

She shoots him in the face.

THE END

www.ingramcontent.com/pod-product-compliance
Lightning Source LLC
Chambersburg PA
CBHW032206190626
46810CB00018B/1873